The Other Sister

Helen Bland

G_h

The right of Helen Bland to be identified as the author of this
work has been asserted in accordance with Section 78
of the Copyright, Designs and Patents Act 1988

The book cover is copyright to Helen Bland
The book cover image is copyright to www.istockphoto.com
/gb/portfolio/hannamonika

This book is published by
Grosvenor House Publishing Ltd
Link House
140 The Broadway, Tolworth, Surrey, KT6 7HT.
www.grosvenorhousepublishing.co.uk

Disclaimer:-

The characters depicted in this book were born from the author's
imagination. They are entirely fictitious, and bear no resemblance
to any persons, either living or dead.

A CIP record for this book
is available from the British Library

ISBN 978-1-78623-386-8

For Davina and Sara

By the same author:
Painter of the Sacred

Prologue

A Sonnet to Giselle from Gaston

Beware my love of untrue hearts
Of blackened lips reciting vicious lies
Sorcery concealed beneath smiles and sighs
Veiled evil languishes in sombre shadows
Waiting breathlessly in nebulous turmoil
Mesmerising memories disturb your dreams
Whispers of wounds past trail fissures in your heart
Tempered passions hold us close
Sensuous hands calm your mind
Binding our bodies with exquisite grace
Drowse not my love our time has come
Beguile our enemies with audacious stealth
Destroy malaise and jealous greed
Recapture tranquillity with sweet honour indeed

List of Characters:

Gaston Villande - Husband of Giselle
A beguilingly sexy French art and antique dealer in his late thirties, of average height, with dark hair and eyes. He has an adventurously romantic nature.

Giselle Villande - Wife of Gaston
A spirited art historian in her early twenties, tall and lithe with titian hair and green eyes. She is deeply in love with her husband.

Inez Roxberg - Mother of Giselle, estranged wife of Henry
A tall, radiant sculptor and artist now in her late fifties, she shrouds her life's sorrows with life's pleasures.

Henry Roxberg - Husband of Inez, lover of Margot
An elegant, mercurial landowner and art dealer in his late sixties, with luxuriant pale grey hair and hypnotic, piercing blue eyes.

Honoré Roxberg - Daughter of Henry and Inez, younger sister to Giselle
Sporty, competitive and reckless with titian hair and pale blue eyes.
Introspective by nature, she remains submerged in her own personal isolation.

Margot du Val - Housekeeper and Mistress to Henry
A statuesque beauty with captivating blue eyes, in her mid-fifties. Her nebulous persona at times borders on insanity.

Simone du Val - Daughter of Henry and Margot, half-sister to Giselle and Honoré
A capricious malcontent, her exquisite personal attributes do nothing to assuage her perceived loss of birthright. Her ruthless determination to fight for her inheritance proves detrimental to her personal life.

Max - Butler and Valet to Henry
Short in stature and immensely strong, with black hair and pale blue eyes, now in his mid-sixties. Henry's childhood friend from Vienna retains an unwavering devotion to his employer.

Iona Kerr - Cook/Housekeeper
With flaxen hair and blue eyes, at the age of forty-three this well-travelled native of Northumberland returned penniless to her first love, the infinite beauty of her homeland. She has ambitions to dilute then ultimately remove Margot's influence over the household.

Flora Innes - Gardener
A petite, timorous orphan of seventeen, with fair, untamed curls and soft brown eyes. She lives with her grandmother on the estate; her nature is gentle and compliant.

Collette Rouché - Cook at Café Villande
A scheming embittered former ballet dancer, now in her early fifties, and a dangerous predator of the male sex.

Claude Rouché - Son of Collette and assistant manager at Café Villande
Loved by males and females alike, he possesses a flamboyant nature. In his late twenties, his bleached white hair and mischievous, electric blue eyes invite the wrong type of suitors.

Part One
Menton – France 2016

Gaston opened his sultry, soft brown eyes and exhaled a long breathy sigh. Memories of his turbulent dreams returned to disturb his drowsy equilibrium, and lingering traces of a champagne hangover circled inside his head. He relaxed again into a languorous stupor.

It was early morning on a day set aside for relaxation and sensual pleasures, early autumn sun glimmering through the closed shutters, threading his eyelashes with gossamer strands of light.

The room was still. She was sleeping, a lullaby of gentle waves lapping the shore outside their window, disturbed only by the occasional cry of sea birds.

The inhabitants of this busy small French coastal town were also sleeping peacefully under a gauzy veil of early morning sun, on this most tranquil of Sunday mornings.

He lay quietly listening to his wife's breathing, hoping that she would not wake until he was ready for her. His enduring love for her led him to invent varied sexual encounters, to stimulate her body and ignite her senses.

Turning slowly, he gazed upon her beautiful profile, the alluring scent of rose and citrus emanated from her body, intoxicating his mind.

In repose her expression resembled that of a child, concealing her exuberantly forceful nature which he found so exhilarating.

The refracted morning light filtered his vision, relaxed his mind, and calmed his senses.

Paying close attention to his breath, he began breathing in rhythmic unison with her whilst meditating, and focused on her nipples as her breasts rose and fell.

Gaston continued to watch her, drinking in the sight of her voluptuous naked body.

An interval of two weeks had passed since coitus had taken place between them; their tantric practice of abstention served to intensify their lovemaking and resulting powerful climaxes.

Giselle, ever playful, invariably surrendered to her husband's oblique sexual tendencies, his hypnotic arousal techniques mesmerised and excited her more acutely than any aphrodisiac.

She invited his exploitation of her sexual weaknesses, encouraging him to dominate her by removing her physical defences, her husband's intense lovemaking transporting her into a state of endless rapture.

Now, in the distance, he could hear the bell of the Basilica Saint Michel Archange calling the townspeople to mass. Covering his ears, he remonstrated with himself. *Have patience, control your passions*, he thought. Breathing deeply once again, he allowed languor to claim him.

As he lay there, incoherent thoughts of his childhood floated into his head. Would this be the encounter when his wife would conceive a child of their own? She had readily agreed the timing must be his decision, as he was older than her.

His ambitious parents had moved to Menton from Lyons soon after his birth, to be closer to both of their families. Being an only child ensured him of their undivided love and care.

Throughout his idyllic childhood, though, he struggled against their over-protective and sometimes suffocating devotion.

The beach became his salvation, to swim and surf in solitude, escaping the restrictions placed on him by his parents and tutors.

When he was twenty years old his parents had moved away to Paris, establishing their careers as legal notaries and leaving their son in the family home to complete his Master's degree and run their café.

Gaston's passions for art, antique furniture, and coastal waters anchored him firmly at home in Menton. His bachelor years were salacious but uneventful; at heart, he knew himself to be a one-woman man – a conviction confirmed after meeting Giselle.

For him, it was love at first sight. She possessed an air of romance so lacking in his previous girlfriends, and he had immediately been drawn to her coquettish smiles and gestures.

Having just completed her degree in History of Art at the Sorbonne, a chance meeting at Gaston's café prior to her interview for the position as junior curator at a local gallery, was to change her life forever.

He noticed her sitting alone, staring pensively into her coffee, lost in thought. Venturing forth, he placed a tempting pastry before her. She looked up and returned his kindness with a ravishing smile. 'Thank you,' she said. 'How have I deserved your kindness?'

Returning her smile, he asked for her mobile number.

'Hmm, a practiced seducer, I see,' she said, still smiling. 'l will give your request some consideration,' she added, placing his business card in her bag.

The café had many customers that day, leaving him little time to continue their conversation. When he looked back some time later, to his acute disappointment she had gone.

Giselle's interview had been a triumph. Her enthusiasm counteracted her lack of experience, and the director of the gallery appeared to like her, so she was hopeful of being offered the post and to return to Café Villande at Menton.

She called her mother at home in Honfleur to say that she would be home later that evening, but failed to mention that she had met a disarmingly handsome man who would eventually become her husband.

He raised himself to look down upon her. *She is so young*, he thought, *and so completely unaware of the sensual gravitational force orbiting her body.*

In preparation for her waking, he began to flex and stretch his naked body, whilst simultaneously concentrating on his breathing, focusing now on the gauzy linen curtains gently billowing in the salty sea breezes.

His thoughts turned to how he would handle her body this time. A light application of patchouli and jasmine oil to his palms would facilitate smoother stroking caresses along her body, down into her luxuriant groin valley to entice her senses, heightening her arousal and prolonging her ecstasy and ultimate fulfilment.

In an heroic effort to control his arousal, he gracefully arose from her bed, lowering himself to the floor to begin his accustomed yoga practice. The strenuous asanas diverted his mind and contained his lust.

Strong, tanned muscles rippled as he exercised, strengthening his core, restoring his virility, and polarising his mind.

Their previous two weeks of non-physical lovemaking, tantric gestures, controlled longing, and self-imposed abstinence would later be swept away by their mutual acts of exquisite carnal pleasure, releasing the profound joy of mutual orgasmic ecstasy.

Giselle began to awaken. With eyes closed, she smiled provocatively, sensing his presence. Aware that he was watching her, she began stretching and purring then beckoned him. He remained silent and still, his impassive gaze fixed upon her beautiful face. A fleeting smile crossed his lips, and her hips responded with an involuntary motion. His silent, unwavering gaze created heat and moisture along the length of her body.

How long must I endure this exquisite torture? she thought. Mesmerised and breathless, the flames of desire licking her body, she began sucking her fingers one by one to tempt his touch. Still no words were spoken between them; she could have screamed out in frustration.

Gaston often delayed their pleasures, sometimes for days or weeks. There would be no obvious outward sign of his intentions, but her senses recognised the subliminal signs emanating from him. He imagined her as the embodiment of Venus, his mermaid from the sea; he was enchanted by her.

Overwhelmed by lust, he could no longer contain himself and moved slowly towards her bed, the intoxicating scent of her flesh invading his senses.

She allowed his tongue to circle her nipples, and her secret place exploded in ecstasy. 'This is just the beginning, my love,' he said.

The quivering urgency of his arousal had extended his body to a throbbing fullness. She reached for him, fingering his urgency with a featherlight delicacy.

Towering over her, his body convulsed with an all-consuming lust, then he lowered himself next to her.

The first touch of her pale silken skin sent a powerful surge of love through him. She turned to him, taking his sex in her hand. Placing her thumb at its tip, she began caressing the area of his lower back, her tantric caresses excluding time and space. She adjusted her thumb slightly to allow a space for her quickening tongue, tasting his essence, then replaced her thumb whilst kissing him with slow deliberation, each exploring the labyrinth of emotions that bound them.

His strong arms held them entwined together as they moved away from her bed, pausing for breath to touch and tease as they moved from room to room. The changing light of the dawn accentuated their secret places, and they took their pleasures in a flowing sexual seclusion.

Taking periodic rest, she languished naked on a pedestal chair draped in faux fur. Smearing carmine rouge onto her fingertips, she provocatively caressed her lips, nipples, and sex, to enhance their colour and succulence.

He reclined on floor cushions to enable his gaze to travel upward beyond her secret place to her glistening breasts, lying as if hypnotised by her presence, intoxicated by the sight and scent of her opulent body.

These infrequent interludes kept them wanting. She ached with unspent passion and longing, and her body writhed in anticipation for the resumption of his manipulation of her.

She became consumed by the heat between her legs, and reached for herself.

He deftly placed a bottle of chilled Chablis against her secret place to cool her ardour; they ate prepared oysters, using their bodies as eating vessels, savouring the delicious morsels from the contours of their bodies.

They drank chilled Chablis as they inhaled and exhaled in twined measured breaths, whilst absorbing the sight of their perfumed naked bodies, focusing on their every gesture and enticing movement.

The air now laden with the hormonal scent of sex and expectant tension drew them together, enveloping their bodies as they entered the first poignant affirmation of their union.

Gaston carried her into a capacious marble bathroom. The swell of the waves reflected through the French windows onto the mirrored walls as they lazed in scented water, regaining their strength to continue until satiated.

As the tide turned, they imitated the ebb and flow of the waves with the motion of their bodies, which served to extend and control their pleasure.

Carved, coloured glass bottles containing scented oils intended for pre and post copulation massages were arranged on glass shelves. *Secret of the Desert* for her; its alchemy consisted of pheromones, rose oil with a hint of citrus. Gaston had a preference for his own infusion of nutmeg, lime leaves, and cardamom; these augments heightened their senses and soothed their soreness.

Their final release infused their bodies with spiritual feelings of a near-death experience.

When at last they awoke, the moon was already casting its silvery beams across the sea, across the beach, into their consciousness. They had slept for the remaining daytime hours.

Giselle was first to wake. She looked in disbelief at the clock. *Our day off and we slept through it*, she thought.

Stroking Gaston's feet, she whispered, 'Wake up, darling, the day has gone.'

He sighed and turned away. 'I feel drugged. What did you do to me?' he said.

By now, Giselle was wide awake and felt completely revived. Rising, she tied her long hair into a braid then slipped into her robe, shivering in the early autumn chill.

Crossing the room, she paused before the open door leading to the roof terrace.

The seductive little town lay before her, the narrow streets and village square again deserted at this hour. She could hear a dog barking.

'Gaston! Gaston!' she cried. 'Where is Maude?'

He shot out of bed, grabbed his shorts, and made for the stairs. Claude had left her in an unused pantry with water and food, and she was clearly disgusted at missing her walks. She nipped him on the ankle when he released her.

Tourists filled the town during the summer months, children played on the beach with their parents, lovers lazed or sat and talked in intimate bars and cafés.

Giselle worked long hours in the café, helping Collette and her son Claude to keep their customers happy. Gaston had neither the inclination nor the patience to be of any use; the emporium took much of his time and he was content to leave Giselle to manage the café when her time allowed. Like many local residents, he preferred the quieter winter months when the town became their own once more.

Giselle had grown to love this little town with its wealth of varied food markets and artisan shops. Its perfect location on the border with Italy, close to the cosmopolitan city of Nice, provided an attractive venue for her friends and family to visit.

She sat in their roof garden, drinking her first coffee of the day, and watched her husband accompanied by his precious terrier walk further on down the beach whilst her thoughts meandered back to their second meeting, the one that changed her life.

Her first chance meeting with Gaston had lingered in Giselle's memory, and she had intended to revisit her feelings by calling into the café unannounced.

Keeping her intentions secret, she arranged a short holiday for herself and her sister Honoré, in the South of France. With some trepidation, she booked hotel rooms for them both in the historic quarter of Nice.

The climate was very much to her liking – endless days of sparkling sun, the bluest of skies, together with a variety of art galleries, the opera house, and delicious cuisine, all drew her to that part of the coast.

Two days prior to their departure for home, she found the courage to suggest a visit to Menton.

On the morning of their excursion, she felt tense with anticipation. *Would he be there?* she thought. She was sorely tempted to reveal her secret to Honoré. Such was her dread at the thought of Gaston's absence, she thought Honoré was bound to detect her mood of false gaiety, which barely concealed her true feelings of trepidation and panic.

Undercurrents of sibling rivalry still reigned between them, and she knew her sister would have teased her mercilessly had she learned of Giselle's infatuation.

When they arrived at the café, he was nowhere in sight and Giselle's heart sank. As the waiter walked over to take their order, she noticed him giving her a rather speculative look.

Claude served them with an appetiser, then rang Gaston on his mobile to alert him to Giselle's presence.

He was walking Maude along the beach when he received Claude's call. 'Don't let them leave, I am just a few minutes away,' he said.

He was wearing a long, white linen shirt over his bathing shorts. Feeling hot and sticky, he decided to take a quick dip to freshen his body. Tearing open his shirt, he plunged into the sea and swam parallel to the beach, surfacing opposite the café. Maude ran after him barking furiously, as she disliked water in any guise.

Giselle, ever watchful, heard her barking then saw Gaston emerge from the waves. She felt a rush of raw passion soar through her body as she watched him walk towards them.

Gaston, dripping with seawater, sat down beside her. Raising her hand to his lips and looking deep into her eyes, he murmured, 'You'll not escape me again, my love.'

She introduced him to Honoré who, with a half-smile and raised eyebrows, said, 'Have you been holding out on me, my naughty sister?'

Gaston ordered Chablis and olives for himself and a dessert for the ladies. They laughed and talked for a while then Gaston invited them to dine with him that evening. As they left, Giselle pressed her phone number into his palm. He squeezed her hand in grateful response.

Honoré became increasingly subdued as the afternoon wore on. 'Look,' she said, 'you don't need a gooseberry tonight. I will go back to the hotel alone and leave you to enjoy your evening.'

'You will certainly not,' expostulated Giselle. 'I want you to get to know him.'

That evening, they dined on seafood linguine made with oysters, and lobster flavoured with lemongrass. Copious amounts of champagne left them all feeling relaxed and receptive.

Both girls were seduced by his knowledge of art and culture; his careless, witty elegance and sultry charisma beguiled them both.

As the evening wore on, it became obvious that Gaston and Giselle were seriously attracted to each other. Their unwavering eye contact made Honoré feel so uncomfortable that she decided to take a taxi back to the hotel.

Giselle apologised for her ill manners, kissed her sister, and arranged to ring her the following morning. Gaston was not sorry to see Honoré leave, as he wished to be alone with Giselle.

He suggested a perfectly innocent nightcap on the beach, and they went into the kitchen in search of a picnic. Collette had left for the night. However, having recognised the signs of a blossoming romance, she had prepared a basket containing champagne, two flutes, and dark chocolates; all covered with white linen napkins. She had threaded a soft wrap through the handle of the basket for their comfort.

They walked along the beach hand-in-hand, wishing their time together would never end. Finding a secluded spot, they spread the blanket and lay down.

The sea was calm that night, the air warm and humid. As dusk fell, he took her in his arms, his kisses merging endlessly into each other; she lay back with her arms above her head, allowing his urgent exploration of her body.

The champagne had imbued him with an audacious bravery, and he whispered endearments into her ear as they fell asleep entwined together.

A rose-tinted dawn was spreading her rays over the waters as Gaston opened his eyes. Giselle was still curled into him. He kissed her eyelids to waken her and she looked at him, smiled, and attempted to sit up. He held her still in his gentle grip then, brushing the hair from her forehead, he kissed her, saying simply, 'Darling, I love you. Will you be mine? I want you with me forever.'

Giselle reluctantly departed later that afternoon, wearing a diamond on her finger and a deep conviction in her heart that she had found her soul mate.

Honoré, on hearing the news of their engagement, felt crushed, as Gaston had left her spellbound.

The following day, the sisters separated once again. Giselle returned to her Mother at Honfleur.

Honoré travelled back to England, feeling duped and rejected by her sister; jealousy grew in her like a fruitful vine. *Why does Giselle have everything I want?* she thought. She felt like a wounded dove returning home to roost.

Her over-indulgent father had spoiled her nature with his guilt.

When Henry learned of Giselle's attachment, he insisted the marriage ceremony would take place in their ancestral home. She, however, was incensed at 'these ridiculous outdated traditions'. She stamped back and forth in frustration, muttering, 'Such nonsense! Our family is a perfect model of disunity.' Eventually, with persistent coaxing from her mother, she calmed then acquiesced.

Gaston, ever curious about his fiancée's family and their strange English habits, readily agreed to the venue; his parents would stay at the lodge for a short time prior to the nuptials, to acquaint themselves with their soon-to-be extended family.

His parents' request for a guided tour of the building was met with evasive but firm excuses, preventing them any exploration beyond their bedroom and ground floor. They were advised to come equipped with warm clothes and an electric blanket. Gaston was most amused at this archaic suggestion. *They really are a primitive tribe,* he thought.

When he first glimpsed Giselle's family home – perilously close to a cliff top overlooking the sea, set in a wild untamed landscape of rugged coastlines, long beaches bordered by bogs and meadows – he was initially stunned.

Birdsong from nearby wetlands filled the air under endlessly changing skies; he felt at once what it meant to be at one with the elements. He was impressed by the savage beauty of the terrain but questioned how anyone could survive in comfort throughout the long, dark winters.

Inez, in agreeing to be present at the wedding service, remained adamant in her refusal to allow Margot to attend or have any input in the arrangements. 'A family wedding is no place for a mistress,' she told Henry.

He gave her a mock salute and a sly wink. 'As you wish, my dear,' he said.

Her father's intense dislike of Henry's heartless disregard for his daughter's happiness excluded him from the guest list, much to Inez's relief, as the event was to be a wedding not a war.

Prior to her marriage to Henry, her father had constantly warned her not to marry the womanising scoundrel; however, love prevailed as common sense flew out of the window. Inez would admit to no-one but herself that she still loved him and nurtured her hopes of a sincere reunion. In the meantime, she was happy to comply with his wishes in casting any thoughts of divorce into the future.

Henry had remained steadfast in his refusal to countenance the scandal of a divorce, thus proving her father's opinion of him to be correct. Inez appeared to accept the arrangement with indifferent resignation; she enjoyed living the life of her choice at Honfleur.

In truth, he was trapped with no room for manoeuvre in his relationship with Margot. She ruthlessly maintained her grip, cleverly camouflaged in servile affectations of devotion – a grip that only death would sever.

Inez enjoyed the company of close friends and occasional lovers in France, away from prying eyes, undisturbed by society's conventional notions of respectability and restrictive manners still prevalent in most circles. Her free Spanish spirit needed space to breathe and create her art.

Gaston and Giselle's wedding ceremony took place in the damp, little church which lay just beyond the walled garden in the shadow of tall pine trees; their boughs shaped by ferocious westerly winds.

The autumn sun beamed its pale golden rays into the tiny chancel, now festooned with white orchids and ferns. Peonies grown by Flora, the estate gardener, stood sentinel at the entrance to the vaulted porch.

Henry proudly walked his spirited daughter down the short aisle to join the man of her dreams; Honoré, as bridesmaid, followed behind wearing a long dress the colour of *eau de nil*, her eyes downcast and disconsolate. Only Simone knew of her secret longing for Gaston. She had lost… Giselle had won his love; she had been overlooked again.

Honoré, during their visit, had shunned her mother's every attempt at conversation. Inez had tried in vain to reach her daughter, to explain why she'd abandoned her, but Honoré refused to listen. She would never forgive her for leaving her in a cold and draughty mausoleum of a house with a mostly absent father and his volatile housekeeper.

Gaston's father had readily accepted his son's invitation to be his supporter, and envied his choice of wife.

They were all perplexed at Henry's choice of priest, as they had expected a member of the local ministry to officiate. Instead, they were presented with a stranger from Vienna. Gaston resolved to ask for evidence of his ordination after the ceremony, in order to confirm the validation of his marriage.

Inez's father had taken him aside over a brandy or two the previous evening, and had explained the little he knew of the family's skeletons. Looking around, Gaston wondered how many more were still lurking in the family cupboard.

Giselle wore a long sheath dress of ivory crepe, cut in folds to her waist at the back, with pearls stitched around the neckline. Her understated jewellery consisted of the diamond engagement ring given to her by Gaston after their second meeting in his café at Menton.

His heart soared as he placed the platinum rope twisted wedding ring on her finger. 'Now you are all mine forever,' he said.

The wedding feast took place in their candlelit dining room and was a lavish family-only affair. A Venetian crystal chandelier shone like stars above their heads. Silver cutlery lay at their fingertips. Henry was the perfect host, helping Max and Flora to keep the champagne flowing and pre-dinner canapés offered to their guests.

Seven courses, each accompanied with wines appropriate to each delicious course, were served on the finest Sèvres china.

Iona had cooked and baked until her arms ached, but had somehow found time to make a traditional wedding cake, decorated with sugar flowers identical to those in the chancel of the church and the bride's bouquet, surrounding the base with nature's greenery.

Conversations around the table were affable and polite. Seemingly innocent enquiries regarding Henry's line of business were met with courteous but evasive responses.

Gaston had his own thoughts on the subject of his father-in-law's line of business, as it was fairly obvious to him that Henry's apparent wealth was not sourced from his largely unproductive estate. Perhaps he would make a few discreet enquiries of his own.

Margot was conspicuous by her absence. When Inez enquired as to her whereabouts, she was informed by Henry that she was visiting relatives who lived abroad. 'Another time then,' she said.

Inez knew that Margot was of French extraction, unless of course she was masquerading under a false name; anything was possible, given her scheming nature.

Henry was treated as lord of the manor by his staff, however he had been duly ostracised by his neighbours when it was discovered that Inez had deserted him due to Margot's malign influence.

Iona lived in the village. Unbeknownst to the household, she provided the most rampant of village gossips with snips of information in an attempt to undermine Margot's position. There was no love lost between the two women. Iona would take any opportunity to be the architect of Margot's downfall.

Henry, like his father before him, had made no useful contribution to the local economy or taken any interest whatsoever in their political or village affairs, preferring to live in his crumbling lodge in a permanent state of isolation with his family and staff.

Max regularly drank in the local pub and, whilst sitting quietly one evening over a pint of lager, heard the exaggerated rumours and speculation regarding his master's lifestyle.

Margot and Simone were both utterly *persona non grata* to everyone, their reputations as gold-digging harpies avidly discussed amongst the female members of the community.

Giselle thought her family so dysfunctional that she just wanted to get married then leave for France at the first available opportunity.

The newlyweds had been married for just four months when Giselle heard the tragic news of her sisters' accident.

They had been skiing together off piste when an avalanche hurled them both down a mountain.

Fortunately, the interval between the accident and their rescue was short. They were airlifted to a hospital in Switzerland, where the staff experienced some difficulty in identifying each sister due to their disfiguring facial injuries; the two not only resembled each other, but shared the same blood type and were also dressed in similar clothes.

They were both immediately placed in induced comas, allowing dedicated medical staff time to fully investigate the extent of their injuries.

During the first night, one sister died, whilst the other hovered on the brink of death. After three weeks, the medical staff cautiously reported to Henry that his daughter Honoré would survive.

Three painful operations and months of physiotherapy failed to restore her to any semblance, both mentally or physically, of her former self.

The once highly competitive sportswoman had gradually descended into a well of bitter self-pity, becoming increasingly withdrawn and frail.

Giselle had written to her regularly but had never received a reply. Her telephone calls had been deterred with persistent hostility from Margot.

Gaston, at times, found her lamenting tiresome. 'Please, Giselle, just go. Arrive unannounced. They won't turn you away, after all, she is your sister.'

She deliberated and brooded then rang her mother, and Inez eagerly agreed to accompany her. She had missed Giselle's bright company since her marriage, more than she cared to admit, and would look forward to spending time with her. Henry might even be out of the country on business, leaving them to their own devices.

When Giselle had rung off, the painful memories and events she had suffered in her former marital home came flooding back. *Yes*, thought Inez, *it's time I confronted that witch Margot.*

Inez had purchased her pale blue beachfront villa at Honfleur when the difficulties in her marriage had begun to surface. It had become a refuge since Henry had thought to continue his affair with Margot. *Why, why,* she thought over and over again, *did he marry me when he had her?* Although, she had long since resigned herself to the unpalatable truth, that her only attribute in his eyes was her wealth.

Feeling the need for fresh air on her face, she donned her coat and boots then headed outdoors to the beach.

A fine early evening mist hung over the estuary, the air was fragrant with wild thyme. Sun-dried lavender spikes punctuated the edge of the beach, the fading light lending them the luminescence of icicles. Fishermen's boats had been moored for the night, the sky was a pinky grey, noisy seabirds had fallen silent in their roosts. As she walked on aimlessly, her thoughts evoked a picture in her mind of the lodge as it looked prior to her marriage.

She had paid for extensive restorations to the fabric of the building and the construction of the gardens.

The building that so impressed Gaston was almost unrecognisable from the one she had moved into in the first days of her marriage to Henry.

Then, the austere monument to all thing Viennese was in a sad state of disrepair.

Constructed in stone and granite, it perched perilously close to the edge of a high cliff overlooking the North Sea on one side, steep steps led down to a spit of a beach. Deep wooded valleys surrounded the lodge, forming natural barriers to the outside world.

High sea-facing turrets pierced the skyline, telescopes were fixed at the windows in order to scan the horizon. Clouds of intrigue and suspicion, like mythical tendrils, suffocated this eyrie of manifested evil.

For reasons that he would never discuss, Henry's preoccupation with his privacy bordered on obsession.

The entrance to the lodge was sealed by black iron gates, beyond which guard dogs patrolled in order to deter trespassers and alert the occupants of the lodge of potential danger.

Built in the late medieval period, these sombre walls had over the centuries heard the echoes of prosperity and debt, love and loss, childbirth and death. However, in more recent times its forbidding walls had heard the screams of imprisonment and torture.

Labyrinthine corridors and the many unused rooms where Honoré and Simone had played, hiding from their tutors and the house staff, had been all they had known until their teenage years.

Henry had long ago forfeited his right to an exclusive relationship with his new wife, his flagrant and persistent infidelity had insidiously eroded their relationship. Margot would constantly creep around the house like a slithering serpent.

Inez would turn to find her close behind, literally breathing down her neck and asking, 'Can I help you, madam? Do you require anything, madam?' This drove Inez to distraction and gradually undermined her confidence. Henry accused her of paranoia and absolutely refused to discuss the matter.

His continental business connections regularly separated them, and as these separations became more frequent, a self-protective indifference began to grow within her. This drifted into a divisive living arrangement that was painful to them both.

Henry maintained his family dignity in turn and, with some reluctance, she returned to her previous bohemian existence as an artist and sculptor.

As time passed, she chose to accept his sophisticated view of their alliance – for their daughters, she would tell herself; if only she believed it.

Their superficial respect for this uneasy truce allowed them an insightful ease of semi-coexistence, however the hate and resentment between Inez and Margot lay simmering under the surface.

Henry's close relationship with his housekeeper had been forged prior to his marriage, but persisted and was maintained in the face of his young bride's innocence.

Two years had passed when came the realisation that her husband's unexplained absences were more than just estate business.

One dark winter evening, Inez found him in the kitchen with Margot sitting in his lap. The housekeeper was in much distress as she had just received confirmation of her pregnancy and knew Henry did not want a child with her. He had said so often enough.

Inez, pregnant and almost full term herself, was incandescent with rage.

She insisted that Margot must leave and take up residence with the father of her child; not then realising that her husband was indeed the culprit.

Henry pretended to consider her request. 'After our own baby is born,' he said.

'A suitable replacement would be difficult to find in so short a time.'

Inez, her suspicions aroused, kept a watchful eye on the visitors to the vast kitchens with their numerous anterooms and pantries. The painful discovery of her husband's infidelity was replicated many times over in the weeks to follow.

Margot had found it impossible to contain her own spiteful nature.

She had been devastated when young Master Henry married Inez, the daughter of a wealthy Spanish industrialist friend of the family. Her prospects of great wealth, combined with her exotic beauty, had been an irresistible combination and Henry did not resist.

Margot as a young girl loved to cook. She sat at her French grandmother's table, avidly absorbing intricate methods of cooking classic French cuisine.

She possessed looks and ability, but alas no money. As she grew into womanhood, her manipulative nature would be employed to entrap a wealthy husband.

Margot occupied rooms in the west wing, overlooking wooded glades. The view extended to open countryside where birds of prey soared over trees and up into the high towers above the lodge.

These bright, sunlit rooms were well known to Henry, as he had spent most nights with her prior to his marriage. Their adulterous liaison continued in secret until that fateful night of their discovery.

Margot's role as housekeeper placed her in the unenviable position of having to arrange her lover's wedding breakfast and accept his usurper bride into her domain.

She was ultimately forced to masquerade as a widow, but the villagers had their suspicions as to the identity of the child's true blood father.

This seed of ill content grew within Margot. She had given herself body and soul in devotion to Henry, only to be overlooked as unworthy. Year after year, as her child grew into a lively, well-educated young woman, she plotted, watching and waiting for an opportunity to rewrite history.

For now, she would content her revenge by administering insidious doses of belladonna poison, infused from plants grown in the kitchen garden.

Margot's cruel intention to terminate Inez's pregnancy failed completely, due to the other woman's timely departure for France.

Henry's refusal to allow both girls to live with their mother, forced Inez to abandon her eldest child, Honoré, in favour of her unborn child.

At least she will have her half-sister for company, she thought despondently.

Honoré and Simone, as children, had been both inseparable friends and enemies alike. They were educated together in the schoolroom in the north wing of the lodge. As winter gales blew, the window casements overlooking the sea rattled so fiercely that it frightened the two young girls, who imagined the spirits in the lodge were angry and would punish them for their wrongdoings.

Honoré would not venture alone into the upper hallways after dark. Simone, though, had no such fears. She played spiteful tricks on her half-sister, such as hiding her treasured dolls, reading her diaries, or placing white mice or insects in her dress pockets to disrupt their lessons, causing their tutor to punish them both by issuing additional after-study tasks.

Honoré, as she grew, missed Giselle so much that she often crept into her father's study using his telephone to call her, later incurring his wrath when the account was presented.

At mealtimes the distinction between staff and gentry was most apparent.

Simone invariably ate in the warm kitchen with her mother, whilst Honoré dined upstairs with her father when he was at home.

Giselle and her mother were close confidantes. Giselle felt a deep sympathy laced with anger for her mother's situation, and a deep admiration for her stoic endurance of the tragic marriage.

Her sister, Honoré, lived a life of pampered comfort with their father, who employed just enough loyal staff to enable their comfort.

Henry's butler, Max, was a rather stocky man of robust proportions, condescending in his manner to perceived underlings and villagers alike, which endeared him to no-one. His questionable choices of female companions invited derision, and even Henry teased him mercilessly on the subject of his love life.

Max had previously made inelegant advances to Flora, the gardener, who was young enough to be his daughter, and to whom on everyone depended for their daily fruit, vegetables, and fresh flowers

Iona, the cook housekeeper, had soundly slapped Max's face and stamped on his foot when he attempted to slide his hand down the front her dress late one evening. She was revolted by his assault on her person.

Being a well-travelled astute lady, having experienced life at the sharp end, she placed a high value on her settled employment and would not stand any nonsense from anyone, least of all Max

The reins of restraint, where Margot was concerned, were at times stretched to breaking point as she fought to conceal her dislike, occasionally through narrowed eyes. She could often not contain herself from expressing a barbed criticism here and there.

Margot was extremely possessive of Henry, and at times he found her claustrophobic attentions too much to bear. They were, for the most part, suffered in silence, as her usefulness in the bedroom had not diminished over time.

The household ran along smoothly in the Edwardian style of living, where luxury was commonplace and taken for granted. This extravagant existence proved alien to Inez's nature, as she found it increasingly suffocating. Feelings of isolation overcame her as she became resistant to her selfish husband's behaviour.

Occasionally, she would invite Henry to stay with her in France, on the genuine pretext of his wish to visit Giselle and in the hope of separating him from Margot on a more regular basis.

He never accepted her invitation; his rejection of her was complete. She would continue to seek solace elsewhere.

Her home at Honfleur constantly overflowed with interesting and attractive cultured types, who her husband considered vacuously pointless.

Inez found the situation hard to accept, but nevertheless she was determined to remain in their marriage of convenience for the sake of her daughters and the destructive love she still felt for her husband.

Giselle, however, would not have tolerated this arrangement in her own marriage to Gaston. Their passions were constant and insatiable; she bound him to her with the invisible threads of her sexual generosity.

Café Villande, unbeknownst to its owners, was carefully managed with a furtive licentious disregard for faithful and honest relationships.

Liaisons between close friends or lovers, married or otherwise, were encouraged and arranged with discretion, and the staff recompensed.

Claude, the waiter and co-manager, passed notes or spoken messages to errant husbands and adulterous wives. The intoxicating combination of delicious food and carnal desires were persuasive bedfellows to the inhabitants of this overheated small French town.

Claude gained great satisfaction from his employment. Quite frankly, he would move in and reside in the café if it were possible.

A short fellow, unusually blond for a Frenchman, enhanced the allure of his blue-grey eyes with a little shadow. His manner was as coy and theatrical as his clothes were flamboyant, in both cut and colour.

He would sway between tables, dispensing overt acid wit or endearments, then retract his comments if they had given offence.

His devotion to older men occasionally led him into difficulties, as they pined for him so. They found his delectably promiscuous nature so appealing.

On occasions, he would find it necessary to hide in the cellar, if his duplicity had been discovered. He sported the occasional black eye, which he covered with a patch to hide his shame, but this rendered him irresistible to some of his male regulars.

He was aided and abetted by his mother, Colette. The quality of her cuisine was well known around the district. Her kitchen, a haphazard den of sorcery and culinary delights, was usually in chaotic disorder, thus concealing the aphrodisiac infusions she made in Gaston's absence.

Customers would invariably order these exotic concoctions with their coffee after dinner. The practice ceased with the advent of Giselle, as she would never have consented to such louche behaviour.

Collette met her many amours amongst the customers in the café. She flirted outrageously with the objects of her desires, only to spurn them at will when she tired of their attentions. She had never married. Claude's origins were her secret and she would not be drawn on the subject; it was possible that even she did not know his father's identity.

With wry amusement, Gaston watched her provocative attempts to ensnare the local men by any method available to her.

A native of Menton, she was acquainted with or related to many of its inhabitants. An avid diary keeper, no-one was exempt from her scrutiny.

She constantly fantasised about would-be lovers, however her sly nature eventually repelled most interested parties.

This left her with feelings of resentment towards her more fortunate female acquaintances, the jealousy consuming her and impairing her judgment, while inside she was slowly withering. Her false charm and voracious sexual appetite beguiling her unsuspecting suitors disguised her utter contempt of men.

Still lost in thoughts of her family, Inez suddenly felt chilled. It was now almost completely dark, so she turned and began to jog home to warm her body, if not her heart.

When the newlyweds returned home after their wedding, they spent two blissful weeks together. Gaston drove her around the towns and villages closest to her new home to familiarise her with the area. He encouraged her to redecorate their private quarters above the café to her liking. Her happiness was his only concern.

Giselle's new contract with the gallery would begin in January. As the month of September had just begun, she had three months to acclimatise, so she threw herself into her new life.

She had an interest in interiors, and her painting skills were as accomplished as any professional designer. She began by transforming their apartment and Gaston's antique emporium.

Gaston was most particular in his assertion that they must have separate bedrooms with their own bathrooms; this appealed to his romantic sensibilities and sexual preferences. But Giselle had not slept in her own room since moving to Menton, preferring to stay close to her new husband. On one occasion, Gaston found it necessary to stay overnight when away on business, and she decided to try her own bed for comfort.

On the night of Gaston's absence, she felt lost and lonely. The café had closed, Claude and Collette had returned home for the evening, and she was left alone.

A bath and book, she thought, *the perfect cure*. When she eventually snuggled down with her book, feeling relaxed and fragrant, she felt something scratch her face. Running her hand carefully over her pillow, she found a tiny stone – a blue opal.

She was puzzled. Perhaps Collette had a piece of jewellery with a missing stone? She would ask her tomorrow. Placing the stone in her jewellery box for safe keeping, she returned to her bed, an unfamiliar musky scent of patchouli and bergamot floating up from the sheets as she fell into a dreamless sleep.

She awoke the next morning to Gaston's kisses. He had arrived during the night and slept in his room so as not to disturb her.

It was Sunday, their only completely free day together. After breakfast, they walked with Maude and made love on the beach.

He was enthralled by his new wife. She fulfilled his every expectation of marital bliss. She told him about the stone and saw his expression change. Although he liked his staff, he was not sure that he trusted them. 'We shall see,' was all he said.

The next day, as Giselle was helping Collette in the kitchen, she drew from her pocket a handkerchief containing the opal she had found in her bed.

When Collette saw the stone, her face suffused with colour, but she denied any knowledge of how it came to be in Giselle's room.

That evening, she rang her sister. 'Margot, you fool,' she expostulated. 'What were you thinking? Dispose of that ring,' she told her. 'There must be no evidence that you were here!' She was shouting now. 'Your careless disregard for our plans could ruin everything!' She slammed the phone down and poured herself a glass of wine.

Margot ignored her advice. Henry had given her the ring and she would not be parted from it. *Anyway*, she thought, *they will never be allowed to come here. If they do, they will die.*

Part Two
Paris

Early morning joys. Gaston's preference was to walk the beach with his terrifying terrier, Maud. The invigorating salty air and restless encroaching danger of the tides and ocean currents fired his imagination as he jogged in the shallows.

His drenched linen shorts clung to his powerful body as he waded close to the water's edge, becoming at one with the seascape.

Inspirational photography and watercolour painting, mostly seascapes, absorbed his spare time. He took images of the venues he visited on his worldwide business travels, and they often became the subject for a painting. He would carry several cameras on his journeys to capture a moment in time worth his attentions.

His artistic temperament was inclined to the great outdoors, and he was often seen painting on the beach in all weathers, wearing his battered, rouge-coloured oilskins.

Giselle displayed his paintings in the café. Her customers often purchased them before the paint had dried. She had encouraged him to expand his horizons and exhibit further afield, but he resisted her suggestions, preferring to sell in the locality and paint at his own leisurely pace. 'Antiques are my priority,' he would say.

His days were spent in the emporium, which was conveniently situated next to the café. Customers would spend hours dining and browsing his varied items of furniture and paintings. The rapidly-expanding business regularly took him abroad in search of unique pieces for his collections.

Maude accompanied him on his business journeys throughout France, however he would not consider taking the little madam abroad, as chaos and disruption would ensue. Her annoying habit of nipping other, usually large, dogs had cost him a fortune in vets' bills or bribes to their outraged owners.

He missed her terribly when his work took him to countries unsuitable to her wellbeing or theirs, though! She was his favourite subject, and he drew rapid sketches whilst attempting to keep her still.

Maude would gambol amongst the dunes whist he painted. She would tackle any dog twice her size if they were caught invading her territory, her bite being worse than her bark.

She would cautiously stalk the object of her dislike and attempt to nip its behind, then run like a hare and hide under Gaston's easel, adopting a well practised look of innocence on her face.

She was now eight years old and arthritis had started to claim her joints, which might explain her intolerant short fuse where other dogs were concerned.

Gaston loved the bitch to distraction, and constantly turned a blind eye to the more unsavoury aspects of her character, remarking to all that allowances should be made in respect of her age.

Walking on the beach early one morning, he called to Maude as he turned to retrace his steps back to the café. His journey led him back along the path toward the rear of the café. He noticed the door was open and Maude shot in front, scenting Claude, her compliant supplier of tit-bits.

He crept over to investigate, and caught sight of Claude leaving by the side door, arm-in-arm with his latest catch.

Gaston called to him, 'My friend, when do you sleep?'

Claude turned with a sly smile on his face and called back, 'I live for love, my friend.'

Gaston went indoors and raced up the stairs, where he prepared a breakfast of strong black coffee, ripe fruit, and home-made yoghurt. When Giselle appeared, he recounted the episode to her whilst attempting to conceal his amusement. She was most displeased, for it was not the first time Claude had entertained his latest amour on the premises. She would speak with her errant manager to remind him that this was not a house of ill repute.

She was unaware that Claude and Collette had cultivated a lucrative sideline in ensnaring unsuspecting marital deviants, assisting in their adulterous arrangements when required.

Blackmail paid rather well and particularly suited Colette's passion for wreaking revenge on any man who crossed her path, not to mention men in general.

On one unfortunate occasion, a couple of marital swingers disclosed their deceptions to other diners, then proceeded to pass notes around other tables warning potential miscreants to beware of the staff at Café Villande.

When Giselle discovered their infamy through a close friend and informer, all hell blew up! She hit the proverbial ceiling in rage and disappointment at their dishonest behaviour.

Dismissals were discussed but never issued. Gaston employed every ounce of charm and persuasion in his possession in their defence, as in his bachelor years they had supported him in his effort to make the café a viable concern.

By increment, he reconciled his differences with Giselle. They all wore velvet gloves around her thereafter, but she was not fooled. From then on, she kept a vigilant eye on their activities; never again would she place her complete trust in them.

Claude and Collette were diligent staff in all other respects. Gaston knew that in his absence the exacting standards he considered essential to smooth the café's path to success would be met or exceeded.

Collette invented a new menu each week, and her passion for delicious cuisine was unwavering. Their many customers often commented on her elegant table décor and spotless presentation; in truth, he could not afford to lose them.

Claude, unlike his mother, had an open sunny nature. Likened to a beautiful butterfly flitting from his subjects of interest to his people of interest, he would talk endlessly about the happy childhood he spent with his grandparents on their farm at Ypres.

Their olive grove and market garden provided a rich cornucopia of fruit and vegetables, cheese, and poultry. They converted part of the farmhouse into a small bed and breakfast holiday let, which proved useful to visiting family members out of season, and Claude in particular.

Paying guests received a warm welcome, gloriously fresh food, and sumptuous wine, and were disinclined to leave once ensconced. Some regulars visited several times a year.

This rural idyll was perfect for Claude's occasional visits to dry out, unwind, and catch up with family news. But he would become restless after a week or so as the sophisticated city night life drew him back to Nice.

Collette was closed and secretive. Her observant eyes missed nothing, her inquisitive mind a trap waiting for a suitable opportunity to capture her victims.

She absorbed information like a sponge, her memory likened to a well-thumbed encyclopaedia of people and their personal lives.

She succeeded by employing insidious methods of verbal and mental intimidation on everyone she met, and turning false gaiety on and off like a tap in order to camouflage her true feelings.

Initially, male customers found her physically attractive for a while. But eventually, when their flames of infatuation were eventually extinguished by her spiteful nature, they lost interest then deserted her.

She was a native of Menton, having lived there all her life. Local people remembered and told the story of her mother, who had given birth to twin daughters.

One day, she left them alone in the market whilst perusing the stalls. On her return, she found that one child had been stolen, reportedly by travellers.

The profound grief she felt at losing her baby through her own neglect weakened her mind and drove their father away, leaving the mother doubly bereft.

Years later, her mother took a new husband and moved to his farm, leaving

Collette, who was now old enough, to live a lonely existence in her childhood home. She avoided questions about her early life or always gave evasive answers then changed the subject.

At times throughout her employment at the café, Gaston had plied her with champagne in an attempt to engage her in conversation about her childhood, but his enquiries proved futile as she simply would not be drawn on the subject.

When the parted sisters grew into womanhood, and with the advent of the internet, they found each other again. Gaston often thought it strange that he had not been introduced to the sister or even knew her name. But he dismissed it lightly as being none of his business.

Women's instinct told Giselle that Collette withheld untold secrets, and on several occasions she had felt the weight of the other woman's speculative glances. Collette even offered to clean their apartment or change their sheets. Gaston considered these suggestions were a kindness to Giselle, but she would have none of it. Collette left her feeling strangely uncomfortable.

Gaston managed his antique business without assistance. He disliked professional interference, maintaining that it diverted his creative flow. Bric-a-brac and collectibles did not interest him either, nor did he have the space to store them.

He travelled the world attending auction sales, clearances at chateaux and country houses, in his search for unusual items of furniture or paintings.

His emporium was imaginatively arranged in room settings, and he preferred to offer a personal service to his customers.

His clients would often seek his advice on the subject of interior design and the placement of their furniture.

This he found boring and tiresome, as he had no interest in his clients' soft furnishing.

Invariably, he breakfasted at leisure outside his café, with Maude at his feet waiting for the odd treat. He could be seen concentrating on his laptop whilst soaking up the sun or watching his neighbours going about their daily tasks

Collette would whisper local scandal in his ear however unfounded or salacious it later proved to be. Her verbal embroidery was legendary around the town, but it amused him to listen to her tales.

She suffered from an addictive attraction to Gaston, but she went to great lengths to conceal it, in order to stay close to him. She had offered herself in the past but he had always managed to avoid her advances.

Collette had never searched her soul for the origin of her discontent. Sadly, she constantly stood in her own sun.

Giselle liked to dine out on most evenings, as the kitchen in their apartment was inconveniently tiny. Being the lucky recipient of her mother's imaginative culinary arts since childhood, had spoiled her interest but not her palate.

In her short lifetime, she had tasted the most exquisite *cordon bleu* dishes at home at her mother's table; only after she had married did she realise the deficiencies in her own culinary skills.

They would dine at one of the many varied restaurants which Menton had to offer, and everyone knew the couple. Gaston sometimes found their lack of privacy irritating, as an intimate dinner was often his prelude to lovemaking.

They often drove down the coast and over the border to San Remo, where they would dine undisturbed and unnoticed.

The sedate family atmosphere of this Italian town provided them with a tantalising escape and yet another beautiful beach to explore.

Gaston's romantic sensitivity was easily aroused, thus keeping their relationship light and fresh. The dark undertones of his nightclub bachelor lifestyle were cast aside in favour of intimate evenings with his wife.

Giselle would usually dress in her favourite pale silk, floating chiffon dresses, which lent the delicacy of a semi-naked Sabine. Her slender limbs moved with the fluidity and caprice of a ballerina, her dainty feet shod in the flimsiest of coloured leather footwear.

Gaston abhorred underwear, preferring to savour the line of her body as she moved without restraint. He gained some satisfaction from the thinly-veiled attention she received from other men. She was fully aware of her narcotic allure and used it sparingly.

Occasionally, they would travel to their chosen venues separately, as if they were strangers meeting for the first time. Giselle never tired of their games, as she was always intrigued to know where they would lead her. She trusted her husband and his inventive pathways to pleasure.

Gaston, like most businessmen and women these days, regularly updated his website with his latest pieces when convenient orders were shipped abroad to his customers. Gaston preferred to deliver his furniture in the local area if possible, preferring to build his customer base with a kiss or a handshake.

Since his marriage, he had kept an ear to the ground in the hope of hearing something of Henry's contacts.

He imagined their paths would cross from time to time, in view of having similar business interests. This was not to be the case. Conversely, when he mentioned his father-in-law in passing to other dealers, they flatly denied any knowledge of him and moved on. Eventually, he stopped referring to him, as their association might adversely affect his own business.

Gaston had, unbeknownst to Giselle, offered his hand in friendship to Henry on many occasions in the early years of their marriage. His genuine requests had been referred to Margot, Henry's human shield, who informed him in plain terms that they had no time for visitors.

To Giselle's distress, all communication between herself and her own family had been brief and perfunctory since her marriage. She wanted to visit Honoré and offer her help.

Gaston viewed the situation with mistrust laced with disgust. He decided it was time to pay his father-in-law an unscheduled visit, but wondered if Inez's father could shine a light on the matter first.

Waiting until Giselle was lunching with girlfriends in Nice, he rang Inez's father in Seville and arranged to meet him in London the following week.

They met for lunch inside a discreet hotel restaurant. Gaston was soaked, as he had left his umbrella on the plane. He looked up at the leaden sky and offered up a silent prayer of thanks for the Cote d'Azur. Inez's father had aged considerably since they had last met. He explained that he was suffering from an illness that was slow to grow, and extracted a solemn promise from Gaston to keep his secret.

Inez had sanctioned their conversation. Her father told of his horror when she had revealed her intention to marry Henry.

He had remonstrated with her in the months prior to her nuptials. In desperation, he'd offered financial inducements, and recounted rumours with regard to Henry's questionable business dealings with international art dealers, his consorting with continental prostitutes, together with a wilful disregard for money which had led him to near bankruptcy.

Gaston was so appalled by these revelations that he lost his appetite and drank too much wine. When they parted, he went search of a burger bar to absorb the alcohol and quell his hunger.

Inez's father had failed to inform Gaston of the substantial regular payments he made to his son-in-law to ensure he maintained a distance from Inez, his only daughter.

Were she to discover evidence of this arrangement, she would in all probability never speak to him again, not realising that he might have saved her life.

After an uneasy night then brunch with an old school friend, Gaston hired a car and set off for Roxberg Gate. He arrived at the hotel in the village just in time to bear witness to an increasingly violent thunderstorm.

Tree branches were hurled like straws, and local television news advised schoolchildren and adults alike to remain indoors until the storm had exhausted itself.

He settled into his room then rang Giselle to confess his sins. Hoping to avoid her wrath, he revealed his location with extreme caution, but nothing prepared him for her vitriolic reaction. He was forced to hold the phone at arm's length as 'apoplectic' didn't even begin to describe her rage.

Long after her verbal cannons had been fired and she had been persuaded to his point of view, he went down to dine alone and rehearse his arguments for the following day.

The promise of a long weekend together in Paris, on route to visiting her mother at Honfleur, had been intended as his surprise, not a peace offering.

Nature's fury had not disturbed his sleep, but the storm had reportedly caused structural damage and left flooded roads in its wake.

He woke refreshed and ready to demolish a full English breakfast. Five blissful years had passed since his marriage to Giselle had taken place at the house he was about to visit. *What would he find there?* he wondered. His purpose was to save Giselle the shock of any radical change that may have taken place in the intervening years, not to mention the deterioration of her now disabled sister.

Giselle, sensitive by nature, had in effect been born and raised as an only child who could never understand the physical separation between her parents. *They were friends, so why did they not live together?* was her constant mantra.

Gaston drove slowly up to the gates of the lodge and pressed the intercom button. Some ten minutes later, when there had been no answer, he began despairing that his visit would have to be aborted before it had even begun.

In his impatience to gain access, he decided to skirt the perimeters of the estate looking for an alternative entrance, unaware that he was being monitored by Max, who had failed to recognise his master's son-in-law.

Fortunately, Iona knew him at once, so Max gathered the dogs together and locked them up. *He will be back,* he thought.

Such was Gaston's tenacity, he found an adequately-sized fox run under wire fencing roughly half a mile from the main entrance.

Removing his outer garments, he placed them in a waterproof bag and threw them over the fence. It was no struggle for him to wriggle through the gap. *l knew that yoga practice would come in handy sometime,* he thought. *They must grow large foxes in these parts, though.* He brushed himself down and dressed, then walked back in the direction of the lodge.

There were no cars parked in the courtyard, no welcome from the staff.

As he approached, the main door swung open, but still no-one appeared to greet him. Hesitantly, he entered the great hall. The massive door swung shut with such force he reeled from the crash. Hiding behind it was Margot.

She stood motionless, looking at him through narrowed eyes. 'We were not expecting you, the master is away.' She stepped across his path, her evil eyes never leaving his face.

'l came to England on business of my own,' he lied. 'Giselle asked me to convey her best wishes to Honoré and tell her they will be reunited later this month.'

Max appeared at the doorway. 'It is our policy not to admit uninvited guests in the master's absence,' he said, and gestured to the door.

Gaston was astonished at their refusal to even offer him any refreshment. 'This is like a Gothic horror,' he said, raising his voice.

They just stood and stared at him in silence. Max held his arm out once again, in an effort to indicate with some determination that Gaston must leave.

He stepped outside, feeling like a naughty schoolboy. Max said he would bring the car round and give Gaston a lift back to his abandoned car; this was an order, not a request.

Driving along, Gaston turned to Max. 'Look here, this is unacceptable. What is going on?'

'I am not at liberty to say, sir. However, if you have any regard for your own safety and that of your family, do not return.'

Gaston was furious now. 'Damn your cheek,' he said. 'Henry will hear of this.' But Max gave an insolent smile and shrugged his shoulders.

When Gaston arrived back at the hotel, he headed straight to the bar. He was more shaken than he cared to admit. After a hearty meal and almost a bottle of Burgundy, he mused, *Well, that's the first time I have ever been treated like that, and it will definitely be my last.*

When Giselle and Inez learned of Gaston's unsuccessful attempt to see Honoré, their reactions were quite different. Giselle flew into a temper of righteous indignation; Inez just grew increasingly concerned for her daughter's safety.

She emailed Henry and insisted on being allowed to visit Honoré later that month, threatening court action if he failed to comply with her wishes.

Giselle and Gaston arranged to stay with Inez at Honfleur for two weeks prior to their journey to England, enabling them to form a plan of action and enjoy her company, and her cooking.

Inez was overjoyed at the prospect of their diverting company and began making preparations for their comfort.

On the morning of her departure, Giselle hurriedly bade farewell to Claude and Colette, leaving them precise instructions as to menus and opening hours, not to mention good behaviour – and definitely no unauthorised parties.

Precious little Maude would be staying with Claude, as Colette fed her unsuitable tit-bits and attempted to alter her habits.

Gaston had travelled ahead a few days earlier, as he had business in Paris.

Giselle called a taxi for her journey to Nice, where she then boarded the train to Paris. As usual, she had overpacked, so her luggage was rather heavy, but she found a helpful porter who just managed to squeeze her large case into the overhead rack.

The train was full of irritated travellers pushing and squeezing to acquire a seat. The air was stuffy as the weather was unusually hot for early October.

Giselle went straight to the restaurant carriage where she ordered lunch and a large glass of white wine. Whilst absentmindedly picking at her salad, she sighed. She missed her husband's attentive company. Two days apart and she was already pining. Then she admonished herself. *Stop this pathetic yearning*, she thought.

She went back to find her seat and discovered a child asleep there. The carriage was so oppressive that she returned to the bar and ordered a second glass of wine.

The train travelled at such an astonishingly high speed that her excitement increased with every kilometre. She longed to see her mother and was already relishing the anticipation of what the next few weeks' adventure would bring.

Gaston was waiting for her on the platform, smiling broadly. She waved and ran to meet him, leaving her luggage behind. He thought her so disarmingly girlish.

'Darling, I have had the most listless journey. I felt like a sardine, we were all so tightly packed.'

Eager to be alone together, they walked off down the platform holding hands. He nuzzled into her and whispered, 'I have more surprises for you, my love.'

He had booked a secluded table at her favourite restaurant, and hotel accommodation close to the Sacré Coeur in Montmartre.

'Two days and nights of pure pleasure,' she said, dancing around him. 'I am so happy. Tomorrow we will visit the Musée d' Orsay, the next day the Louvre.' She leaned in and kissed him passionately.

He smiled indulgently and held her at arm's length. 'Patience, my darling. Save yourself for later.' They hailed a taxi and sped off to their hotel and checked in.

Their room had a curious rustic charm; the bath was situated in the bedroom under the window that faced the street. Giselle just looked at it in amazement.

'Is this hotel designed for exhibitionists?' she said.

'We can bathe under the stars,' replied Gaston.

Sweet strains from a lilting violin floated up through the open window. They looked out onto a tiny market square. Stalls selling jewellery, candles and garments, were surrounded by people avidly discussing the merits or disadvantages of the goods offered for sale.

Market traders sat under drooping umbrellas in the leaf-strewn square, chatting idly, drinking wine, and singing loudly to the music. As the sun sank slowly towards the horizon, it sent low beams of luminescent amber through the almost bare branches of the trees, giving them the appearance of ghostly fingers as they swayed in the gentle breeze.

Dimly-lit cobbled streets lent an air of mystery and excitement to their evening stroll. Giselle loved Paris.

She could hardly wait to walk the streets to absorb its romantic atmosphere.

Gaston closed the lower window shutters and ran a bath for them both.

Giselle lay on the bed with the intention of ringing her mother to advise her that they would be late in arriving, two days late, but she couldn't face hearing her mother's disappointment. She decided to ring her later or in the morning.

Gaston gathered her into his arms then immersed her in jasmine-scented bubbles. He carefully washed her all over in a most lascivious manner, a lazy smile playing around his lips.

'Could you be persuaded to repeat the sexy welcome you gave me at the station?' he asked, joining her in the scented water.

'It will be my greatest pleasure,' she said as she kissed him.

After taking their pleasures, they lazed in the bathtub, drinking mint juleps and eating madeleines infused with citron, then slept soundly for a couple of hours.

Giselle woke to hear an alert from her phone; she had missed her period last month. She dismissed the screen and the thought of pregnancy. *She was enjoying herself, so why worry?* she thought, and turned over. But sleep evaded her.

The room had grown chilly, so they rose and closed the window, dressing quickly, and decided to walk to the restaurant.

Outside, a velvet darkness had descended, drawing them along the low-lit streets. Just as they were about to enter the restaurant, Gaston paused noticing the figure of a man across the street, standing in profile smoking a cigarette. He thought he recognised the man as a friend of Claude. He paused again, waiting for the traffic to pass, but when he looked the figure had disappeared. Assuming he had been mistaken, they moved on, taking their places at a table near the window.

They were both famished and, salivating at the thought of dinner, they ordered steak au poivre, sweet potato fries and a green salad, and a bottle of luscious burgundy wine, followed by a *mocha vacherin* for dessert.

Giselle failed to notice her husband's distracted expression. The same figure who had caught his eye earlier that evening, was still standing opposite the restaurant.

As Giselle chattered on animatedly, Gaston felt a growing unease. *Perhaps he is watching another diner,* he thought.

'Darling, are you listening'? she interjected.

She continued to discuss their plans for the following day, which included a visit to the Musée d'Orsay in order to view the works of Eugene Boudin, a particular favourite of theirs. They both admired his subject matter, and he was a former resident of Honfleur.

Gaston had previously arranged a late afternoon appointment at Quai Voltaire to view an eighteenth-century walnut bureau for a client. Giselle wanted to buy perfume from the Rue du Faubourg Saint Honoré for her mother, as a peace offering for their delay in visiting her.

They would part for a time to follow their inclinations, arranging to meet later for dinner in Montmartre at six pm. She clapped her hands together. 'We have tomorrow arranged,' she said.

Feeling satiated, they walked, arms around each other against the chill of the evening air, towards their hotel. A gauzy new moon slipped under the clouds which did little to illuminate their path. Giselle clung to him, her mood playful and seductive.

As they turned a corner, the shadowy figure stood directly in their path. Without hesitation, the figure lunged forward, a knife in his hand. Gaston pushed Giselle into the road and shouted, 'Run, save yourself!' But she screamed, transfixed to the spot.

Gaston raged and turned attacker, lunging forward. There was a struggle and he lifted his knee, striking his attacker so violently in the crutch that the man dropped the knife, wrestled free, and ran off.

A gendarme had heard Giselle's screams and came running to their aid – too late to catch the perpetrator of the crime.

They both stood utterly stunned by the incident. Gaston was too shocked to give chase, which in any event would have entailed leaving Giselle alone and unprotected. He was unhurt apart from a bruised arm and ego, but unanswered questions invaded his mind. *Had this been a random attack or a motive-driven plan?*

Giselle assumed the man was drunk, but privately Gaston had other thoughts which he would keep to himself for now, not wanting to frighten her.

Recovering his composure, he tried to calm Giselle with humour and vacuous conversation, but his mind was racing. He was sure he recognised the man as the figure who had been watching them when they left the hotel earlier that evening.

On entering the lobby, Gaston searched his pockets then discovered his wallet was missing, together with their room card. Fortunately, the hotel reception was open around the clock, so they would at least be able to access their room.

Giselle had the necessary funds to pay their bill. They sat in the bar until a late hour, recovering from shock. They resolved at least to try drawing a line under the evening's events, preventing it from spoiling the plans. But Gaston's private feelings of impotent rage lingered on. The incident had left him severely apprehensive and thoroughly unsettled.

Giselle was convinced it had been a drunken, random attack, but her valiant efforts to lift her husband's menacing mood were to no avail. He became quiet and lost in his own thoughts.

Could it be…? No, they would never go to such lengths, he thought. *Unless they had much to lose.*

The following day dawned bright and sunny, and the Parisian autumn air imbued them with its seductive charm.

Gaston tried in vain to put the incident of the previous evening behind him so as not to spoil their day, but he felt a simmering undercurrent of resentment toward his attacker that he could not cast aside.

He would ring Claude later to discuss the matter and enquire if all was well at the café. He encouraged Giselle to join him in a short yoga session. He was the more practised devotee; since her marriage, she had half-heartedly joined him on occasions, whilst he considered the asanas essential to his daily life.

They breathed and stretched in controlled unison for thirty minutes then bathed together. They achieved their objective, their polarity now in balance, minds and bodies calmed and now restored.

After a breakfast of fruit and coffee, they caught a bus to the Champs Elysees and strolled down through the Jardin des Tuileries, fox-coloured leaves whirling around their heads in a brisk autumn breeze.

At noon, they caught a taxi to the Musée to engross themselves in its treasures. She bought a book to add to their collection; Giselle often read for hours at home in the evening, sitting on the roof garden of their home.

Gaston left at 3pm to keep his appointment whilst Giselle made her way to Hermès to buy perfume for her mother, and perhaps herself. Gaston rang later to say that he was in a taxi and would collect her from the Rue du Faubourg. Truth to tell, he was nervous of letting her out of his sight.

When they arrived back at their hotel, Gaston went to the reception desk to arrange dinner while Giselle went on ahead to run a bath. As she walked along the hallway to their room, she was shocked to find the door to their room was ajar.

Thinking perhaps the housekeeping staff were still servicing the room, she tentatively pushed the door open. Her eyes widened in disbelief at the scene of utter devastation that was their room. Someone had indiscriminately emptied the contents of the closets and drawers onto the bed and floor.

She fainted away in shock. When Gaston arrived a few minutes later, he was faced with the scene of his wife sitting on the floor being comforted by a male guest who had happened to be walking down the hallway at the time.

The manager of the hotel called a gendarme and they were asked to remove themselves so as not to contaminate the crime scene. After an initial inspection, the forensic team took their fingerprints in order to eliminate them from their enquiries.

Naturally, the gendarmes would inspect the cctv footage for clues as to the burglar's identity. They asked Gaston and Giselle if they had been involved in any arguments recently or had any known enemies, as at first glance nothing appeared to have been taken.

When Gaston informed them of the attack of the previous evening, he was made to feel uneasy, as if the gendarmes were regarding him with slight suspicion.

'Are you withholding any other information, monsieur?' they inquired.

Their increased scrutiny made him feel almost guilty, as he had mounted a counter-attack on the man. His thoughts kept returning to Max and his warning threats.

When the gendarmes had gone, the manager arranged for their belongings to be moved to an alternative room.

Gaston was bewildered and incensed by this latest incident as it had started to resemble intimidation. Neither of them felt sleepy, so they went down to the bar for a drink.

The following morning, the manager informed them that the lock on their bedroom door had been accessed by the usual card method. So, clearly his attacker had been a random thief and pickpocket of some considerable skill.

This welcome news went some way to alleviate Gaston's fears that Henry's staff were somehow implicated in some way. It later transpired that, as they thought, nothing had been stolen. Giselle pleaded with her husband to forget the incident and just enjoy their day at the Louvre.

The beautiful gallery was surprisingly empty when they arrived, and Giselle went into raptures at almost every picture, describing the meanings of symbols and subject matter together with sentiments they conveyed.

Her enthusiasm for her subject never once wavered for the whole day.

She is a natural teacher, he thought proudly. Later, they walked on to Notre- Dame to offer up a silent prayer for their safe deliverance from their attacks.

The street cafés that lay at the foot of the cathedral coaxed them invitingly into dining early, as they had missed lunch.

The enchantment of the city seeped into their consciousness. As they dined, Gaston's thoughts turned to tantric carnal love. It fed his soul and intensified his love for Giselle. Looking out over the tranquillity of the Seine, he yearned for the turbulent beauty of the sea and its coastline.

The next morning after breakfast, they departed from Paris to begin the tortuous journey to Le Havre, where Inez would be waiting to collect them.

Gaston was nervous and watchful. He could not help himself. He was fearful of yet another incident, as next time it might involve Giselle.

Part Three
Honfleur

The pretty little French port of Honfleur lies beside the Seine estuary in the Calvados region. The temperate climate is similar to that found in the far south of England. Quaint towns punctuate miles of sublime coastline, drawing artists, photographers, and lovers of gastronomy from all parts of the world to its shores.

Inez had carefully chosen her place of self-imposed exile for its beauty and ease of transport connections, thus enabling her swift return to Northumberland if the need arose.

Henry's cruel insistence that Honoré be prevented from visiting her mother and sister at Honfleur remained a constant vexation to both of them during Honoré's formative years. 'Margot will perform the duties of motherhood in your absence,' he would say time and again. 'She is happy enough without you creating a disturbance her life.'

Oh, how Inez hated him, loved him, whatever. He clouded her transient relationships with other men and constantly invaded her dreams. *Would she ever be free of him?* she wondered.

When looking upon Giselle sleeping peacefully in her bed, she mourned the absence of her first daughter and nurtured the hope that in time they would be permanently reunited.

Henry had considered it unfair that Simone should remain isolated at Roxberg Gate without the company of both half-sisters, though his failure to acknowledge Simone as his own flesh and blood secretly infuriated Margot. She held her composure with a degree of dignity whilst secretly plotting to remedy the situation by any methods available to her. She would watch and wait; the time would come to tighten her grip then execute her plan.

Henry, Honoré, and Simone would visit Giselle on her birthday, and a table would be booked at a restaurant in Rouen, as Henry habitually declined an invitation to La Maison Bleu.

When Giselle was enrolled as a weekly border at a school in Paris, his visits became more frequent as he found it easier to avoid Inez. Then as she grew into a spirited independent young woman, he found her criticism of him an embarrassment and began to distance himself. Being a cosseted only child, he had not learned to accept the opinions of others; above all, only his mattered.

Their father-daughter relationship had gradually dwindled until there was just a veneer of polite tolerance, covered by a resentful layer of dust.

Giselle had been an apt pupil, who worked studiously to gain a place at university, concentrating her efforts on her new life of study and socialising with her fellow students. Her family in England became increasingly distant to the point that she hardly thought of them until her late teenage years.

Inez, in contrast, threw open the doors of her home, transforming the rambling, pale blue villa into an exhibition space and summer art school.

She had studied painting and sculpture in Madrid and had qualified to teach young adults seeking further education abroad. She advertised her courses in appropriate journals, she was astonished at the response she received.

Her tall villa faced the estuary, with far-reaching views to the port of Normandy and beyond. The light lent itself to diffused seascapes and portraits using loose brushwork and abstraction.

Although well known to the townspeople, Inez had not lived there long enough to be considered a true *honflurais*. When out shopping in the local food markets, her neighbours would greet her with enthusiasm, engaging her in news or gossip on local issues.

Off they would go with smiles and farewell waves, but she was never invited to their evening soirées or luncheon parties. This upset her as she was made to feel an outcast. She was at her loneliest during the endless winter evenings.

A male friend suggested she join a group of like-minded artists who met in Rouen once a month and often stayed for an occasional weekend. The society did much to alleviate her melancholy. She made a female friend who had experienced similar events in her own life. They were so alike and shared a wicked sense of humour. Inez found it easy to confide in her, as she had much to impart.

Her neighbours were unaware that she had heard their unkind assertions regarding her private life. Inez continued to wear her wedding ring and made no secret that she was estranged from her husband. Still, they spied on her and her students from behind the safety of their shutters.

They assumed that her marital status and gregarious personality would attract the more sexually liberated of students, and their unfounded prejudice prevented her from being accepted by the influential married women of the town.

What did she care? Let their envious tongues wag, she thought. *She had a business to run.*

From Easter to Michaelmas, Inez gave tuition in painting and sculpture.

When the renovations to the main villa had been completed to her liking, she turned her attention to the large orangery that sat at the end of her garden.

She spent endless time and money transforming it into a studio. The doors drew back to allow the bracing sea air to penetrate the minds of her laziest of students.

Drawing and watercolour classes were held upstairs in the old drawing room, as the light was perfect for most of the day. It was warmed by the sun, which suited the life models who would sometimes pose unclothed for the students.

Courses were residential, either weekly or occasionally a whole term, depending on their subject matter; her students were many and varied, the age requirement ranging from eighteen years to infinity.

Initially, Inez advertised her courses in English and European magazines, however as time moved forward and as her reputation grew, her students came by recommendation only.

Some of her more confident male students would attract her licentious attention then fall in love with her. They would perhaps enjoy a brief interlude together, if she so wished, as she considered passion – unrequited or otherwise – an essential element in enhancing both the appreciation and execution of art in all its forms.

These fleeting encounters were a panacea for her deeper fears and constant longing for a more permanent relationship. Her love for Henry had blurred but had not been entirely extinguished.

Inez would never disclose her age to anyone; she held the belief that age truly was only a number. She maintained her lithesome body with gentle daily yoga practice out of doors in calm weather.

The gardener had planted a soft camomile lawn for this purpose, and her supple body and flowing movements caressed the fronds into releasing their calming fragrance. As the powerful scent drifted upwards, she took deep breaths to restore her sense of mindful serenity.

Her daily ritual had the opposite effect on some of her more callow male students; they would set their watches to wake early, then covertly watch her fluid hypnotic movements on the lawn underneath their bedroom windows.

Some would nonchalantly wander downstairs, seeking permission to join her. She sensed their intentions and kept most of them at arm's length. Occasionally, she would indulge herself, if the young man was extraordinary and the mood took her.

Inez had a generous heart. Her serene expression and graceful gestures held a childlike quality, and her shoulder-length red gold hair and translucent skin gave her the appearance of a women in her early thirties, but in truth she was more than two decades older.

The season was drawing to a close and she was feeling the need of respite and to reconnect with her family. Her thoughts, like vine tendrils, were of her daughters and their lives. She would arrange some event that would bring them together.

That morning, the garden was filled with the scent of late blooming roses and herbs, which were grown against a south facing wall for their protection.

Inez, an accomplished cook, used only organic home-grown or local market produce in her delicious menus. A vegetarian herself, she had no objection to cooking fowl or fish for her students or house guests, however she did draw a line when red meat was requested.

Late summer was upon them, the educational year had been successfully completed, her students had all returned home, leaving her alone in her tranquil coastal idyll.

Her home was now fragrant and peaceful, as the housekeeper had worked her usual miracles, the furniture and floors shone, the rugs had returned from a specialist cleaner. The kitchen was the only exception, as Inez preferred to clean it herself.

Guests were allowed to make drinks, but cooking was strictly off-limits.

Gaston had on occasions attempted to assist her, but even he was not tolerated for long.

She had arranged scented fresh flowers in the guest and ground floor reception rooms. A blazing fire had been lit in her sitting room, and the drinks tray filled.

The house was once more her own fragrant sanctuary, and she checked and rechecked the rooms with mounting excitement. Soon they would arrive; the highlight of her year was about to begin. She sat and mused whilst waiting to begin her journey to the airport.

Material possessions gave her feelings of comfort and security. Although she would be loath to admit how much she missed having her husband to share the important milestones in her life, she was becoming weary of temporary romantic attachments with unsuitable young men, and longed for a soul mate to share her life.

Inez had fallen deeply in love with Henry soon after they had met at a friend's wedding breakfast. They had been seated at the same table, next to each other, and the happy day culminated in him inviting her to dinner in London the following week. She had been nearing the end of her degree course in art and design. They fell into deep conversation, rudely ignoring the other guests seated at their table.

He was a seemingly respectable landowner who had inherited a modest country estate on the death of his father. The dilapidated property was situated in a remote location, on the north west coast of England. He spent most of his time abroad supervising his business interests in Austria. When she discovered their shared interest in fine art, she imagined their burgeoning relationship becoming more permanent. The young inexperienced Inez was very smitten with this older, mercurial womaniser.

His eyes shone as he described the untamed beauty of the coastline that bordered his home. 'You must see for yourself, very soon,' he'd said. His clear invitation sent a thrill down her spine.

He continued to elaborate about his life and his wish to have children.

Inez, on her father's orders, employed a little more caution. She was an only child and heiress to a substantial fortune.

Her father, a Spanish industrialist, wanted his daughter to attract suitors who loved her for herself and not for financial gain.

Unbeknownst to her, Henry had researched her background and made sure of an introduction. His plan to seduce and marry her, was a precision-planned exercise carried out to perfection.

Inez admired Henry's adventurous spirit. He told of his ambitious plans to transform the lodge by installing a new heating system and thick carpets to protect its occupants from the penetrating northern chill.

Henry had also made plans to develop sporting facilities; new innovative outdoor pursuits were progressing well. He painted a picture of harmonious bliss, his spell was cast, and she fell for every word of it. She had just celebrated her twenty-second birthday and still lived at home with her parents in their native Spain, when not away studying.

It was a brave leap of faith on her part to leave the warmth and luxury of her native country for the uncertainty of a completely new life with a man she hardly knew.

Their mutual friends thought the relationship was doomed to failure due to the vast age difference, Henry being almost twenty years her senior.

Inez checked the alarm on her watch now. Another hour before she needed to leave. She poured herself a weak spritzer and nibbled camembert and black olives. Settling into her chair, she continued to muse.

The first six months of her marriage were indeed bliss; she had conceived on her wedding night.

Henry was genuinely overjoyed at the prospect of a child to brighten their dreary home, and he appeared attentive and considerate.

He tactfully expressed a concern that intercourse might injure their unborn child, and of his intention to abstain until after the birth. Inez had been completely bewildered by his announcement but accepted his viewpoint without enthusiasm. He came to her bed every night, though, holding her in his arms and whispering endearments in her ear.

Her pregnancy took her through the winter months, as Giselle was not expected until April. The weather that year was very wet. 'Will it ever stop raining?' she would recite time after time, even when alone. When Henry was away on business, she wandered the corridors of the house, feeling disconsolate and lonely.

She had lost her mother when only a child and had no idea how to cook or run a house. Henry already had a more than adequate housekeeper, which made her feel increasingly superfluous to requirement.

On fair weather days, she walked the coastline, familiarising herself with the area and its people. She loved to visit the village tea shop and hear the local gossip, or the hotel, when preferring to dine away from the oppressive silence of the lodge. When Henry heard of her visits to the village, he virtually ordered them to cease. His argument was that it was not her place to be on first name terms with his tenants. She thought him pompous and out of step with the modern world, and told him so. But with great reluctance, she agreed to his wishes, knowing full well that she would be found out if she disobeyed.

The impenetrable security system that her father-in-law had installed after the Second World War had been regularly upgraded and was always switched on.

Inez often asked why such a high level of security was needed in such a remote

Location. 'I prefer our privacy to be undisturbed,' was Henry's usual reply.

Inez had been prepared to sacrifice her own blossoming career as an artist, to bear their children and help in running the estate.

She took lessons to improve her English and introduced Spanish cuisine and culture into the household, much to Henry's delight. He loved the heat in her warming spicy dishes.

Their first Christmas together was celebrated in Spain with her father. Inez, grateful for warmer climes and familiar surroundings; Henry, charming and courteous as ever, detected a slight coolness in his father-in-law's attitude towards him. He went to great lengths to ingratiate himself, however the distance between the two men remained cool.

She remembered her father taking her into the garden to explain the new financial arrangements he had been forced to make, in view of new information he had received regarding Henry's financial status.

Naturally, she dismissed his warnings. After all, she was in love and was soon to give birth to their child. She patted her father's hand and advised him not to fuss as she had more pressing concerns regarding her husband's preferences.

Giselle was three months old when it became painfully obvious to her that Henry's relationship with Margot was of a more intimate nature.

While she was pregnant, she chose to ignore the deference he paid Margot, respecting her decisions, consulting her on issues that should have been in Inez's domain. Wisely for one so young, she appeared not to notice her husband's silent devotion to his housekeeper. Admittedly, Margot was seductively attractive, but so was Inez, or would be when her baby bump had disappeared.

Inez wept in private and became more withdrawn and watchful. She could not understand what bound them together, was it love and passion or blackmail?

Her confidence at a low ebb, she decided to buy a holiday home, somewhere of her own; a place to lick her wounds and heal herself.

She travelled to Rouen to stay with a female friend she had met at university, and they spent three weeks together scouring the coast for a suitable retreat.

It was love at first sight when Inez first glimpsed the pale blue-painted house that stood overlooking the estuary at Honfleur.

It was large enough to accommodate the whole family. She thought it would be their perfect escape, and hopefully foster a better relationship between her husband and father.

She could hardly contain her excitement, and sent Henry an image of the property from her phone, then rang the *immobilier* with an offer of the asking price. The property was empty, so she immediately set about obtaining quotes from builders and decorators to style the interiors to her own liking, not thinking that Henry might have liked some input.

Perhaps, she thought her husband would be more attentive if she removed him from Margot's web of influence for months at a time.

The phone rang, startling Inez from her reverie. It was Giselle ringing to say that their flight had been delayed and they would order a taxi to save her venturing out late at night.

Two hours had passed since their estimated time of arrival. Inez calmed her nerves with a glass of chilled Sauternes. She tried again to telephone them but received no response; the calls went straight to voicemail.

It was nearly nine-thirty when they eventually arrived. Gaston, as usual, bought humour to every situation; Giselle always the impatient one, was fatigued and hungry but excited to see her mother.

They had both held numerous Facetime conversations with Inez throughout the year, however this did not quite compensate for the presence of the one person who understood them both and the intricacies of their marriage.

Giselle stood in awe of her mother's artistic achievements and envied her bohemian lifestyle whilst secretly hoping that she would never have the need to replicate it.

Inez had prepared two bedrooms for their use, knowing that her daughter and son-in-law preferred to sleep separately. Their bathroom was on the upper floor, thus ensuring complete privacy. She intended to cater for their every need, in the hope of more and longer visits in the future.

The house exuded an air of restrained order and formality. Inez considered the most important rooms were the dining room and kitchen. She had two sitting rooms – one a private sanctuary for herself, situated at the side of the house with doors out onto an enclosed terrace. The walls were painted in the palest of sea green. The sumptuous upholstery was covered in a watered silk fabric of a similar hue, and the furniture, much to

Gaston's private disgust, was painted old white. Large Flemish tapestries clothed the walls with scenes of Impressionist paintings. This blend of colour lent an air of much-needed mindful tranquillity, far away from her students and the world in general.

The second sitting room overlooked the rear garden, a large cosy room with overstuffed sofas and armchairs for her guests and students to relax in.

This more vibrant room was decorated in a subdued mustard yellow and old white check. It had an atmosphere of youthful exuberance, tempered by the addition of Inez's own watercolour scenes of Normandy sunsets.

The room had two double doors that opened out onto the south-facing garden and was mainly used by her students. She kept a fire lit in the large fireplace for them to congregate around in the evenings to discuss their day or read.

Overflowing bookcases lined two walls; their varied subject matter would not have seemed out of place in the reference section of a municipal library.

Where possible, produce from her kitchen garden or the local markets were cooked to perfection by Inez herself. Simple but nutritious dishes were served to her students in the dining room. Inez would discreetly correct their table manners if required. Good and sometimes controversial conversation was encouraged, but formality was observed without exception.

Tonight, she would serve lobster in an avocado sauce, with thyme and lemon potatoes *a la boulangère*, followed by pear *flaugnarde* with lime yoghurt.

They all had such an appetite for food and conversation and, although the hour was late, it did nothing to deter them from lingering over their meal.

They laughed and reminisced over dinner, then moved to the yellow sitting room where Inez had lit a fire.

After a brandy or two, they reluctantly decided that sleep was needed if they were not to ruin the following day's outing to Rouen.

Giselle felt exhausted but restless. She needed the comfort of her husband's warmth and scent to calm her. Putting on her wrap, she crept silently along the hallway and up the stairs to the top floor. On entering the room, she found him sound asleep. As she slid in beside him, she leaned over to whisper in his ear, 'I love you,' but he did not stir. She snuggled up to his warm body as sleep swiftly overcame her.

The next morning Inez felt a glow of maternal pleasure as she saw them race downstairs to breakfast. They ate berries with yoghurt, and croissants filled with smoked salmon and scrambled eggs. Gaston had missed his early morning run and needed his daily fix. He knew the day had been planned in advance and that shopping was on the menu.

'Now, ladies,' he said. 'Surely I won't be missed today amongst your female activities.' And with that, he took off through the back door like a frightened hare. Giselle and Inez looked at each other in amazement.

'He's escaped,' said Giselle, and picked up her phone to give him an earful.

They heard his phone ringing upstairs, and both women giggled. They would be gone by the time he returned, and he had neither a key to the house nor his phone to ring for help. 'Hmmm, serves him right,' said Giselle.

They had ordered a taxi with the intention of spending the day in Rouen, indulging themselves in lazy discourse, eating, drinking, and shopping.

They found their coats and handbags, then rang to prompt the taxi driver.

Gaston, by this time, was at the far end of the beach with no money or keys and, more importantly, no phone.

The day was warming up, but the early autumn chill made him shiver.

He went into a café and explained his predicament to a friendly waitress of a certain age. She eyed him speculatively.

'Are you homeless, monsieur?' she asked. 'I have a spare room to rent.' She raised her eyebrows and gave him a sly smile.

'Fortunately, I am not homeless,' he said. 'My wife has locked me out and gone shopping.'

'Well,' huffed the waitress, 'what a poor excuse.'

She returned after a few minutes with coffee, croissants, and her home address. Gaston thanked her, with a promise to return with payment the following day.

At least the natives are friendly, he thought, as he ate his second breakfast of the day.

He often wondered if Inez took the occasional lover; she never mentioned having any friends of either sex. He felt she was wasting her life waiting around for Henry to shed his snake's skin and behave himself. She deserved better, much better.

Occasionally, he would tentatively broach the subject of her personal life, but she would look at him quizzically then smile. He would tease her by offering to buy her a nun's habit for a birthday present.

Giselle would raise her eyes and move away in embarrassment; she thought the subject of one's parents' love life should remain unspoken, unless a conventional arrangement evolved.

One day, over a glass of lunch time rouge, Gaston's discreetly persistent questioning revealed that there was no man in her life, nor was there any prospect of one.

'You forget, my dear, I am still a married woman,' she said.

Naturally, he was unaware of the transient involvements she enjoyed with her male students. No doubt he would have been very interested to hear of her conquests. *Well,* she thought, *he can mind his own business.* She then went into the kitchen to chop nuts.

Inez thought random relationships were the safe option for a married woman whose husband was a permanent resident in another country.

Giselle and Inez decided to dine out in Rouen that evening and return late to La Maison Bleu. Unbeknownst to them, Gaston had risked his neck by climbing into the house by way of Giselle's bedroom. He would give them both a pep talk on home security when they finally returned. They found him sound asleep in the yellow sitting room, an empty bottle and a clean plate by his side.

Inez took herself off to bed, while Giselle kissed her husband awake.

The following morning, Gaston arose early. He dressed quickly for his habitual morning run then, creeping silently downstairs, put a small bottle of water in his pocket and opened the side door of the house. He stepped out, closing the door softly behind him so as not to wake the sleeping occupants. *This is the best part of the day,* he thought, as he headed towards the beach.

The luminous early morning light of a pinky grey dawn bathed the shoreline, blurring the horizon where the sun and sea merged together.

At times such as these, he missed the company of his naughty terrier Maude, who was probably missing him, too. *Hopefully she would be on her best behaviour*, he thought, like children often were when their parents left them with friends or relatives. He resolved to ring Claude later to check on her.

He spoiled and cosseted her as you might a child. Perhaps they should remedy this. A new addition to the family would be a diversion, although he was still not convinced that it would be a beneficial one. Perhaps Maude should have a male partner? Yes, puppies would be much more to his liking.

Gaston looked up and prayed for the promising weather to be kind. Alternatively, cold and dry would do, then there would be plenty of time later for sketching and painting. He was unfamiliar with this part of his homeland and was keen to draw every scene he viewed. They had planned to stay for three weeks, which would include a short visit to England somewhere in between.

He ran on lost in thought. The sea, sky, landscapes, and light in this region were entirely different from the softer terrain at home in Menton, where the bright light defused colour at various times of the day. The intense heat in summer left the landscape parched and exhausted.

He suddenly realised that he had run further than he anticipated, and turned towards home. He was hungry, and the coins in his pocket rubbed his leg as he moved. The café he had begged coffee from yesterday was still closed. Perhaps Giselle would deliver the promised payment to save the waitresses further embarrassment, as he had duly discarded the note of her address.

His morning run was not a method of distancing himself from his wife, as she often thought, but his daily personal regeneration where he collected his thoughts, put his world to rights, and made plans for their future together.

The morning chill was lifting, the day was beginning to warm a little, the breeze had ceased, and the previously scudding clouds now floated over his head like angels' wings.

Back at La Maison Bleu, Giselle was showering and awaiting her husband's return for breakfast. Inez had given her housekeeper three weeks' paid holiday. She was a treasure in the house and very kind in nature, but she was apt to eavesdrop.

She was a native 'honflurais' and had a wide circle of friends in which to share her snips of gossip. Discretion was not her forte, and could not be relied on.

They needed to discuss in private their carefully planned visit to England, as neither of them had seen Honoré since her accident some five years earlier.

Their urgent enquiries regarding her recovery were deflected by Margot, who was reticent and evasive when questioned. Henry just echoed her words; he obviously had no idea how his daughter fared, as he hardly ever saw her.

Inez had emailed Honoré many times and had suggested using Facetime to catch up with her news. Invariably, though, she would decline the suggestion by repeating the same excuse, that her injuries were so disfiguring that it would upset her mother to witness them. This caused Inez much distress, and she despaired of ever building a relationship with her daughter.

Henry suffered Honoré's moods in silence. His pity for her was such that he merely complied with his daughter's wishes, then let the matter drop. His business interests both at home and abroad monopolised most of his time, leaving none for his family.

But storm clouds were gathering. Giselle would no longer tolerate his indifference. Her intention to intervene on behalf of her mother was growing stronger as time passed. The ever-present ghosts in Henry's past were gathering, compelling him to listen to his conscience or pay the ultimate price of death.

Gaston passed a florist's shop on his return from the beach. He stepped in and bought small sprays of autumn crocus for Inez and Giselle, leaving them next to their breakfast plates. His thoughtful gestures melted the hearts of every female that he encountered.

He burst through the kitchen door as Inez was making cheese soufflé omelettes for breakfast, with a side dish of tomato and shallot salsa.

Her strong but fragrant coffee was a daily triumph. He quietly treasured his mother-in-law and envied her culinary expertise. He resolved to visit her more regularly in future.

'Where is Giselle?' he asked. 'We need to decide on dates for our trip to England.'

She appeared just then as if bewitched, with her hair soaking wet and wearing his new shirt. He chased her up the stairs in order to retrieve it. It was some time before they reappeared, looking rather sheepish.

After breakfast they all wandered along the seafront to explore what the town had to offer. They lingered over an early lunch. Inez, as always, derived so much pleasure from their easy company; they spoke freely on most subjects. Gaston held opinions on all of them, and was unafraid to voice them to anyone who would listen.

Lazy days came and went. Giselle had borrowed her mother's library card and had read two books by the end of the first week. Inez had attempted to teach Gaston the method of making pottery, with hilarious results, as he spent most of his lessons wearing the damp clay that he had attempted to fashion into a jug. The resulting vessel would not bear scrutiny, even from a child.

She looked on indulgently whilst he tried to keep the clay upright. He was hopeless, his grip was too soft. *Lucky Giselle*, she thought, as she walked away leaving him to clear up the mess.

Tea-time was the highlight of Giselle's day, as she loved cake… any type or flavour was acceptable, she would even avoid lunch in order to indulge her sweet tooth.

Of course, she limited herself to consuming it, as she was not remotely interested in making it for herself. She was an effervescent young creature and everyone delighted in her company, but she disliked cooking with a vengeance.

Gaston had spoken with Claude several times in the past week. Seemingly, all was well at the café, although Maude had been rather temperamental where her food was concerned. She persisted in barking up the stairs every morning for her accustomed walk with Gaston, and looked most dejected when he failed to appear. This sad news plucked at his tender heartstrings. He would definitely buy her a mate soon after arriving home, but he would take her with him to choose her own companion.

Inez set about booking tickets for their channel crossing and flight to Northumberland. She hired a car for the duration of their stay, then informed Henry of their intention to visit Honoré the following week.

This time, she would not tolerate any denials or vacuous excuses. As a precaution, she had engaged the services of an English solicitor to reiterate her demand for access to her daughter. She was utterly determined to explore every legal avenue open to her, so resistance on Henry's part would be futile. She knew that any mention of the law would send him into a spiral of panic, and relished the thought of his discomfort.

An only child, Henry had been sent at a young age to live with his paternal grandparents in Vienna. He grew up in a repressed atmosphere where the formality of a bygone age still prevailed, and secretly adopted their far-right political views as his own, a view his parents also instilled in him.

In the early days of her marriage, Inez had heard whispers of her husband's dark past and the parents she had never met. At the time, she banished any criticism of him from her thoughts, thinking it was no concern of hers.

Her father had mentioned that rumours and suspicions abounded regarding the family's extensive private art collection. In view of his daughter's involvement with the family, he had made it his business to make discreet enquiries about the validity of ownership with regard to certain paintings.

He discovered vague or incomplete documentation and questionable provenance. Auction houses would refuse to provide evidence of purchase or sale. When she recounted these rumours to Henry, he dismissed them all as pure fantasy.

The gauzy late September sun hovered across the estuary, onwards towards the port of Normandy and beyond to the open sea. Gaston and Giselle watched its progress whilst lazing close together on the beach. He turned to her, saying, 'My love, I will arrange a late evening picnic for us before the weather breaks.' He caressed her cheek as he spoke, his steady gaze spoke volumes.

When they arrived home, he mentioned to Inez that he would like to build a fire and cook a romantic supper on the beach for himself and Giselle. Inez caught his eye and smiled.

'l will invent a menu and provide the food and wine. I have no doubt that you will provide the other pleasures.' Her blatant comment took him completely by surprise.

'l will do my best,' he said with a wink.

With this in mind, Inez began planning a host of epicurean pleasures, leaving her son-in-law to provide the carnal variety.

She decided on a rustic menu of rosemary-infused pork escalopes, as they would cook quickly, together with whole courgettes stuffed with basil and tomatoes, a salsa of caramelised apple and celery, followed by a plump fig and orange liqueur tart to warm on the fire. A bottle of excellent Burgundy wine would complete the feast.

Gaston, seeking solitude, decided to take a long afternoon nap or alternatively immerse himself in a book. He texted Giselle with his invitation to dine that evening, gave her instructions as to where on the beach she would find him at the appointed hour, and suggested she wore a long dress and a voluminous cloak. Prior to leaving with his basket filled with ingredients for their supper, he left a glass of cognac on her dressing table to warm her body against the night chill.

He took no cutlery, as they would eat as heathens at a pagan feast. He imagined the delicious juices flowing down their arms and into their clothes.

The beach that evening was quiet, the light fading into an auburn sunset. Still warm sand stroked his feet as he walked to a secluded curve in the rocks.

He had taken care to read the tides to avoid becoming stranded, or worse, as they might fall asleep after copious amounts food and drink.

Inez held her precious daughter at arm's length to look at her before she left the house. She kissed her, then stood watching as Giselle floated away into the distance like a beautiful spectre. She rang Gaston to say his wife had departed.

Gaston had been collecting driftwood for his fire; the wood was now very dry, and lit easily. Giselle would see the beacon of flames, of course, but not the flames enclosed in his heart.

He sat patiently staring into the fire and waited. All thoughts of home and business had dissolved into the flames as he looked longingly in the direction of the house. Would she tease him? Would she keep him waiting.?

At length, she emerged, her cloak parting in the light breeze as she walked slowly towards him, her hands thrust deep into the pockets of her cloak, shielding her breasts but allowing him provocative glimpses of her semi-naked body. He could detect her musky rose scent as it merged with odours from sea, evoking his mermaid fantasies.

He languished in a fur blanket and she saw that he was naked, apart from loose underwear. He held out his arms to her.

'Come,' he said gently, enfolding her in his arms. He kissed her passionately then poured a glass of wine for them both.

Inez had prepped the ingredients for his convenience and to save time and mess. Gaston crouched over the embers like an ancient savage. With deft movements, he tossed the food over the flames until the intense flavours filled the air.

Giselle could hardly watch lest he should burn his glistening flesh. She savoured the delicious bites of meat that he offered her from his blade.

'Why does food cooked out of doors taste so much better?' she asked.

He laughed. 'It tastes better because I have cooked it,' he said.

When they had finished the main course, they talked for a while about Inez and her life. 'Mother is so tight-lipped about her love life,' said Giselle. 'I feel sure my father is no saint, so why should she not have a little fun?'

Gaston spoon-fed her the dessert course. As he teased the luscious figs between her lips, his mood began to intensify. She recognised the signs. His silent, burning stare sent a glow of warmth through her body, and her nipples hardened as she moved closer, her pulse quickening at his touch. The beach was now deserted; flickering embers from the fire threw shadows, like mysterious pirates stealing ashore with their stolen treasures onto nearby rocks.

They eased themselves further into the velvet darkness of the night. Only the distant sound of revelry emanating from the direction of the town ruffled the still night air. The soft fur blanket sent ripples of pleasure over her entire body as she writhed in the pleasure of his touch, her cashmere cloak forming an exotic tent around them, protecting their privacy.

Suddenly, without a word, he stood up and ran into the water to cool his ardour. He needed to give himself time to layer her excitement and incite her passion.

She watched him emerge from the sea; the mauve twilight accentuated the lines of his muscular frame as he discarded his wet clothes. With no attempt to dry himself, he lay close beside her, his dripping, sea-scented body serving only to increase her lust. She placed the edge of the fur between her legs and slowly teased it back and forth. Flames of pleasure licked at her sex as she began to orgasm, rhythmic contractions of ecstasy consuming her body as he took her with gentle deliberation again and again until their passions were satiated.

They slept awhile then frolicked by moonlight in the cool, salty water, drying each other with their clothes, rubbing vigorously to warm themselves.

Shivering and trembling with cold, they quickly collected the remains of their supper then ran like naughty children back along the beach to the house where Inez was waiting for them. She made a nightcap of hot chocolate containing brandy liqueur, then retreated to her sitting room, not wishing to break the spell of their magical evening.

Truthfully, she was slightly appalled at their dishevelled appearance, as they both looked like vagrants. *Perhaps they played games and fell in the water*, she thought innocently.

Gaston rose early the following morning to take his customary run along the beach. He peeped into Giselle's bedroom to find she was sleeping soundly.

He crept quietly downstairs, carefully avoiding the squeaky treads which Inez refused to repair, as they alerted her to any unauthorised night-time student wanderings.

The kitchen stove radiated a comforting warmth around the room. *Inez needs a dog*, he thought, wistfully imagining Maude racing around this house. *She would adore it*, he thought, *if only she were here*. He made and drank his first espresso of the day, then placed his mobile phone on the table and slipped silently out of the back door. As he walked along the path, lost in thought, he failed to notice a large box on the front doorstep.

The morning sky was grey and a light squall was blowing in from the sea, covering him in a film of moisture. He pressed on undeterred, his thoughts turning to the more practical aspects of their journey to England.

He simply dreaded the unavoidable drama and recriminations ahead of him.

Giselle would constantly lose her vile temper and be upset for the whole time. How he wished they didn't have to go; he loathed family confrontations.

His fervent hopes of their request for hospitality being rejected had been dashed, as no response either way had been received from Roxberg Gate.

No doubt Henry would be filled with unqualified resentment at the mere thought of visitors intruding into his obsessively protected life. *And Margot's bigoted influence would probably extend to the staff*, he thought grimly. He couldn't wait to get the whole unsavoury episode over and return to Menton.

He had thought it prudent to take the precaution of booking rooms for them all in the village, although he had not mentioned this to Inez or Giselle. If the atmosphere at the lodge was unbearable, they may all need an avenue of escape from the ensuing vitriol.

As he walked, his tension increased. The screaming gulls circled the boats in the estuary as they raised their fishing nets, their cries masking the continuous screams coming in waves along the beach from the direction of the house.

A spear of alarm ran down his spine as he turned to where the screams were coming from. For a moment he froze and his blood ran cold as he saw Giselle running towards him screaming, 'Dead! She's dead!'

Her beautiful face was white and stricken with grief, and she fell sobbing into his arms, her garbled words lost in his jersey.

She looked up into his narrowed eyes. 'How can I tell you, my darling, that your beloved little Maude is dead?'

He covered his face with his hands, reeled, then fell to the ground in stunned shock and disbelief. He looked at her in askance. 'It's not her. Maude is in Menton, how could she be here?' he shouted at her.

As they ran back to the house, Gaston's mind was filled with confusion and mounting anger. She tried to explain through gasping breaths and sobs how she had found the box on the front doorstep, containing the frozen, distorted body of his little dog.

Giselle entered through the kitchen. She could not bear to walk up the front path, as the box was still on the front doorstep where she had found it. She went into the sitting room and threw herself onto a sofa, curled into the foetal position, and sobbed uncontrollably, her heart breaking in sympathy for her husband.

Gaston carefully gathered the box into his arms and gently carried it to the summerhouse in the rear garden. He was confused and distraught, and could not believe his eyes. He just sat in stupefied horror at the sight of the rigid, small body of his little friend.

What mind, what person, could commit such an evil act of murder on a defenceless creature? He raged inside. *If the perpetrator had been before him now, there would be two deaths to answer for,* he thought menacingly.

Gaston remained in the summerhouse for the whole day and asked to be left undisturbed. He sat thinking about his past. He had no known enemies, but someone had painstakingly planned this iniquity. Someone who hated him enough to commit murder and deliver it to their door.

That afternoon, he rang Claude, who explained that Maude had been missing for two days. He had assumed she was being seduced, as she had recently come into season.

'I would have rung you,' he said, 'but I knew how distressed you would be. I thought she would come home in her own time.'

Words failed Gaston as he slammed his mobile onto the floor, smashing it into pieces.

Inez took it upon herself to ring Claude back to inform him of the tragedy. Meanwhile, she had contacted the local gendarmes, who visited later that day. Notes were made and images were taken, but Gaston could detect from their attitude that they considered the incident trivial. Meaningless condolences were expressed, and they hoped it was an isolated incident.

At that, Gaston exploded. 'Is that it? Is this all you intend doing?' he glared at the gendarmes. They again expressed their sorrow and departed, saying they would be in touch.

Gaston took Maude's body to the local vet and ordered a post mortem, as he felt it vital to know the cause of death. It was obvious that the dog had been in a freezer, but did she die of cold or something more sinister?

They all spent the next three days in a state of shock and grief. The weight of misery engulfed them, and left turmoil and deep sorrow in its wake.

The vet rang the following day to say that in his opinion the dog had been poisoned with belladonna, and asked if Gaston would collect her remains.

Gaston was so distraught that he was in no fit state to make rational decisions, so Giselle asked her mother if they could bury Maude behind the summerhouse in the garden. Inez found a small antique chest in the attic to sue as a coffin, then lined it with old blankets. Gaston dug the burial space with tears cascading down his face.

After the ceremony, he was inconsolable. The very thought of the journey to England left him feeling unable to cope; deep melancholy had penetrated to his very core.

Giselle's mood was sombre as she rang her father's number. As usual, Margot answered the call. When Giselle asked to speak to her sister, Margot replied that both Henry and Honoré were unwell and unable to come to the phone.

'Then please may I have their mobile numbers so they won't have to?' Giselle replied tersely.

Again, the information was not forthcoming, and Giselle felt her temper rising. 'Will you please inform my father that we will be visiting him next week and will expect to be received. Our party will consist of three persons, one of whom will be his own wife.' To her complete astonishment, she heard the click of the receiver being quietly replaced at the other end.

Giselle returned to the sitting room, her face flushed in temper and disappointment. 'How dare that women exceed her authority!' She paced the room in exasperation, shrugging off Inez's attempts to calm her.

'No, Mother.' She held up her hands. 'I will not stand by and allow the woman who caused you such distress to rule us all!' She threw herself into a chair and drummed her fingers in annoyance.

Gaston poured her a brandy, which was his usual method of pacification if anyone had suffered an upset. Later, when she had calmed, she resolved to thoroughly investigate the situation in England and not be deterred by a supercilious housekeeper.

Part Four
Honfleur continued

Since Maude's gruesome murder, Gaston had become increasingly withdrawn and embittered. His malaise became more unbearable as the days went on, and he would succumb to tears of grief and anger in the privacy of his bedroom, leaving Giselle at a loss as to how to lift his spirits.

His morning runs had become longer and more vigorous, his mind a turmoil of unanswered questions. There would be answers, he was sure of that, and he vowed to severely punish the culprits when they were apprehended.

He rang the gendarmerie every day for a progress report, but invariably he received the same response, being duly informed that they were no further forward in their investigations and still had no idea as to the culprits or their motives; they now considered Maude's murder an isolated incident.

Gaston advised them of his dissatisfaction in the strongest terms, which resulted in alienating the very people who were trying to help him.

As the days passed, he became extremely frustrated and angry at the authorities' lack of interest. 'If Maude had been human, a very different course of action would have been taken,' was his constant theme.

Giselle found her husband's sorrow difficult to cope with; he was inconsolable and nothing she could say would salve his grief. She was inordinately grateful for her mother's supportive company. They spent their days together gardening and reading, in fact, doing anything to avoid Gaston's sombre moods.

Back in Menton, Claude realised that his neglect of Maude would leave an indelible scar on the previously excellent relationship he had enjoyed with his employers. He decided to leave the café when his mother returned from her unauthorised few days' holiday. He would look for employment elsewhere, perhaps over the border in Italy as a means of escape from the beating Gaston was likely to give him when they next met.

He knew it would be impossible to stay, even if they forgave him; the ensuing endless reproaches would be too much to bear. He was also concerned about the reception his mother would receive for having gone away without Gaston's permission, leaving Maude in his sole care. When Collette returned, she scolded him for being too hasty in his decision to leave, and suggested he seek sanctuary for a while with his grandparents at their secluded farm at Ypres.

Claude secretly disregarded her advice. He imagined his fate and he didn't like what he saw. Instead, he gave Giselle notice via email, which she duly forwarded to Gaston. Claude explained that he was too shamefaced to stay on at the café, as he would live in dread of becoming the constant target of their wrath.

Gaston was furious. 'Bloody coward!' he said, as he reached for his replacement phone.

There was no reply, so he texted his instruction for Claude to collect him from Nice Airport two days' hence. If he failed to turn up, Gaston threatened to find him and administer a sound thrashing.

Claude immediately went into a spiral of nervous apprehension. He had been dreading the sight of Gaston's look of contempt and loathing for him, but he gathered his courage and texted one word: Affirmative.

After further consideration, Claude decided against a cowardly escape for his mother's sake, although he was tempted to leave Gaston standing at the airport.

No, he thought, *I must at least apologise for my perceived negligence of Maude.* Even though he still had no idea how she managed to escape from a locked apartment.

Gaston took Giselle into his arms and told her of his intention to return to Menton for a short period. He was apologetic, but also adamant that he felt compelled to make his own enquiries and check if their business was being run as they would wish.

He reassured her that he would join her in England as soon as he was satisfied with the outcome of his investigations into Maude's demise.

At least his delayed appearance in England would enable him to initially avoid bearing witness to any prolonged family arguments. He was sure Giselle could look after herself in that department.

On hearing his change of plan, Giselle sighed, pouted, and gave him dark looks. After a great deal of persuasion on his part, she accepted his motives and reasoning. 'Just a few days, promise?' she said.

He promised, with his fingers crossed behind his back.

Just then, Inez came into the room bearing a tea tray and surveyed them from under her lashes, noting their reticence to speak. She put a match to the fire and served them Lady Gray tea with fresh lemon, chilled fino sherry, warm smoked salmon and herb potato cakes, with apricot madeleines to follow.

'Mother,' said Giselle, 'you spoil us with your wonderful food. I will need to raise my game when we return home.'

Whilst enjoying her scrumptious tea, Inez heard the phone ringing in the hall and rushed out to answer it. As she put the phone to her ear, she heard the unnerving sound of laboured breaths and a voice which she recognised as Henry's.

He sounded in some distress. 'I hear you intend paying us a visit soon,' he said.

'Yes, Henry,' she replied. 'It is good to hear your voice. We are looking forward to seeing you all again.'

Henry paused before speaking. 'I would appreciate your patience and discretion, Inez, as life here has changed somewhat.' And with that, he replaced the receiver.

He must be drunk, she thought, *or someone had a verbal gun to his head.* And she knew perfectly well who that would be.

Inez stood for a moment to compose herself. *What can this mean?* she thought. Henry had sounded incredibly feeble and so unlike his usual ebullient self.

Well, we shall see about that, she thought, as she resumed her cold tea.

Privately, Inez had been quite shocked to hear the weariness and resignation in her estranged husband's voice. *To the devil with discretion,* she thought, relishing the prospect of confronting Margot.

Inez decided not to disclose to Giselle the nature of Henry's request, as she imagined Gaston would have enough to concern him and had no intention of adding to his troubles.

Gaston had been out all day visiting every shop in the town and along the coast, enquiring if anyone had seen or heard anything on the morning of the fatal delivery.

A neighbour told him that she had been walking her dog around six-thirty on the morning in question and had noticed a dark blue hire car parked opposite La Maison Bleu, but could not recall the seeing the driver of the vehicle.

The lady took Gaston's mobile number and promised to try and remember the name of the hire company displayed on the car.

He was beginning to look forward to the solace and privacy of home, instead of wallowing in misery in front of an audience of the two people he loved most. He needed to do something practical, to take his aggression out on someone other than his wife. All of this waiting around was trying his patience to the limit and would not resurrect Maude.

In troubled times Inez always headed for the safety of her kitchen. She began making preparations for their evening meal, giving Giselle the task of making a pudding to keep her mind occupied. They chopped, blended, and tasted the ingredients at their fingertips, each lost in their own thoughts.

When their preparations were complete, they decided to leave Gaston to rest after his day's exertions. Inez poured him a glass of red burgundy and placed a dish of olives on his side table.

Leaving the house by the side door – no-one had used the front door since finding Maude on the step

– the two women walked along the seafront to a small restaurant. The unusually warm evening seemed to invite them to sit and watch the boats hurrying to and fro on the busy estuary. They sat and gazed at the calm luminous water and gave their order of chartreuse cocktails and a dish of olives.

Giselle said for the umpteenth time, 'Only the most deranged and evil person would be vindictive enough to murder a treasured pet. Why?' she kept repeating. 'Where is the motive? What have we done to incur such evil?

She looked imploringly at her mother. 'Gaston has distanced himself from me,' she said. 'He has a barrier that I am unable to penetrate.' He was beyond her, like a stranger in the street.

'Leave him to mourn, Giselle,' said her mother. 'He needs to reconcile his anger, then he will come back to you, of that I am certain.'

As they relaxed with their drinks, Inez suggested they travel to Rouen for a day shopping as a temporary panacea for their troubles.

They had both on separate occasions experienced the severity of a Northumbrian autumn, so a very necessary review of their wardrobes would be an essential part of their physical armoury.

'l am in dire need of warm clothes,' said Giselle. 'Our climate in Menton, unlike yours here, is as far removed from the north of England as it is possible to be.' They paid the bill and pulled their wraps tightly around them. Feeling hungry and a little chilled, they strolled arm-in-arm back along the seafront. The estuary was almost deserted, and the milky softness of the early evening dusk enveloped them.

'l wonder what tomorrow will bring,' said Inez.

'Shopping,' came the reply, 'and lots of it.'

When they entered the house, Giselle called out for her husband. They eventually found him reclining in the summer house, where he had fallen asleep whilst reading a book. He woke with a start when Giselle gently nibbled his ear.

The dining table had been laid in their absence, and a bottle of Chablis was chilling in the fridge. Inez disappeared into to the kitchen and availed herself of a half glass of the well-chilled wine to fortify herself, then added an identical bottle to the rack, hoping that Gaston would not notice.

She served red mullet charlotte dressed with caper sauce, cheese soufflé with ceps and salad. Giselle had made the very grand, apple flan gramaldi, served with cream for pudding.

Inez invariably sought refuge from her anxieties in cooking with the finest ingredients when her students were not in residence. She felt relieved at having a lengthy sabbatical from them all; their constant demands and unsophisticated palates bored her inventive mind. She had avoided accepting bookings for the spring term, so perhaps she would take a year off to travel, re-invent herself, and move on.

Gaston discussed his plans to fly home. He would catch a flight from Le Havre to Nice in two days' time, where he hoped Claude would be waiting with a plausible explanation and convincing answers to his questions.

Next morning, Inez rose early and hastily prepared strong coffee for Giselle and herself, as they would have breakfast later. She was elated at the prospect of a light-hearted day out after the gloom and despondency of the last few days.

She was singing to the radio and belly dancing around the kitchen when Giselle bounced in, and fits of giggles ensued.

Gaston had already departed the house for his usual run, and had left a note on the kitchen table wishing them an enjoyable day.

He was pleased to have the day and the house to himself. With his wife and mother-in-law at a safe distance in Rouen, he had intended to take his pastels and drawing board along the coast to capture the scenic views he may never see again. However, the morning light and visibility were lamentably poor, due to a fine sea fret. *Just my luck*, he thought.

Strengthening breezes and strong currents whipped the turbulent waves, tossing the fishing boats around like champagne corks.

He decided to indulge himself in wild water swimming, as Giselle would be out of earshot for the day. He knew she wholeheartedly disapproved of the dangerous sport.

After coffee, their mood lightened, Inez and Giselle raced upstairs to dress for their day together. Jeans, cashmere jerseys, and smart little jackets under cashmere scarves and flat boots, were their chosen option.

Inez loved to visit the historic university city of Rouen. The vibrant port, with its majestic cathedral, varied shops, and restaurants that catered for every taste, had long ago become her shopping destination of choice.

The city drew them into its atmosphere of old-world civility and charm, with street vendors selling fresh produce and wines of the finest quality. Inez bought various cheeses and two bottles of Gaston's favourite Chateau Margaux.

Tourists browsed the many small shops selling exquisite garments and late season sale items. The convivial atmosphere cured the sadness and cheered their hearts.

'If only this could last,' said Giselle, looking radiant.

Inez led her daughter along the narrow winding streets that were now so familiar to her. Whilst browsing in a department store, they both purchased cashmere scarves and thermal underwear – something quite unknown in Menton, according to Giselle.

Inez, by chance, encountered two female friends from her early days at Honfleur. They had both moved away to Rouen and lost touch with her. The women kissed excitedly and were intrigued to meet Giselle. Immediately, they suggested lunching together to catch up with their latest news. Inez's favourite restaurant was close by, so a quick decision was made.

When settled, the attractive waiter took their order of lobster, French fries, and a green salad, with a bottle of Champagne, of course.

He returned a few moments later with utensils resembling instruments of torture, which caused much ribald mirth amongst those who had borne children. They toasted their reunion and made solemn promises to keep in touch.

Their excited conversation was peppered with half sentences, throwaway remarks and casual enquiries regarding the latest events in the saga of Inez's marriage. They were slightly apprehensive when they learned of her proposed visit to Northumberland, as they both remembered the months of distress that she had suffered after her separation from Henry. She mentioned her art courses in passing, but offered only scant details in Giselle's presence.

The women confirmed mobile telephone numbers and advised Inez that should she find herself in difficulty, to call or Facetime so that they might come to her aid.

It was eight o clock when they eventually arrived home to find Gaston had already dined and packed his suitcase. Inez surveyed them both. Her instincts told her to leave the couple to their romantic farewells, so she quietly retreated to her sitting room, book in hand.

Gaston held Giselle at arm's length. With a look of great tenderness, he said, 'Please understand, my love, we must be parted for a short time. I must find the person who murdered my little Maude. Ensure that your phone is charged and switched on at all times, and resolve your differences with your family.'

He poured them both a generous measure of cognac and placed chocolate nibs in a dish. As she slid into his lap and nibbled his ear, he kissed her head and murmured, 'I will join you upstairs later.'

Taking her hand, he said, 'Come, let's join Inez.' They tapped at her door and it was some moments before she answered. When she did, her tears were flowing freely.

'Dearest Mother, what is upsetting you?' said Giselle, her voice full of concern.

But Giselle soon realised that her mother's tears were of laughter. The friends they had lunched with earlier that day had emailed an hilarious catalogue of suggested retributions for her to enact on Margot and Henry, which ranged from amusing to the unspeakable.

Both friends were divorced from their husbands and harboured extremely jaundiced views of the opposite sex. They considered the majority of men to be just one step away from the cave, but would respond well to training if one remembered that ego-massaging, together with equal measures of excellent food and carnal fulfilment, would suffice their needs and encourage a supplicant acceptance of their role within any relationship.

This attitude allowed time for females possessed of a cerebral nature to proceed unhindered by the domestic expectations of their spouses.

When their laughter subsided, the three looked at each other in surprise. They realised that these were their first light-hearted moments together at home, since the tragedy.

They emptied the vases of their flowers and went out into the garden to place them on Maude's grave. Having avoided using the front door over the past few days, Inez began to wonder if she would ever pass through it again.

Gaston decided to retire early, as he would need to feel refreshed for his journey home the following day. He stifled a yawn and headed upstairs to shower.

Later that evening, when he entered her bedroom, Giselle was fast asleep. He carefully slid in bedside her, the sultry scent and softness of her body inflaming his passion. He wanted her now, to repair the damage and distress he had selfishly caused her in recent days.

He drowned in her scent and felt the familiar warmth of his rising passion. Attempting to restrain himself with deep breathing and meditation, the oblivion that had claimed his wife still evaded him. Eventually, in desperation, he began gently caressing himself whilst gazing on his sleeping wife.

His release came swiftly, and soon after, he fell into a deep and dreamless sleep.

When Giselle awoke the next morning, Gaston was gone.

Part Five
Return to Menton

Gaston arrived at La Havre Airport with a little time to spare, having already checked in online and printed off his boarding pass. He was impatient to begin his journey, but found time to enjoy a reviving double espresso prior to boarding the plane.

He settled into his seat with a feeling of profound relief; he was pleased to be alone with his thoughts at last.

He knew his self-absorbed moods, caused by Maude's death, had exasperated Giselle, but now he did not have to pretend to anyone or fear that he was boring them with his obsessional quest to find the murderer of his dog.

The short flight left him little time to consider his next move. Nevertheless, he was itching to get started.

Claude would be first in the firing line, he thought, as he felt his caffeine-fuelled temper rising at the very thought of seeing the man again.

His flight and landing were smooth and uneventful. Nice sparkled like a precious jewel under a brilliant azure sky, the temperature twenty-two degrees and unusually humid for late autumn.

'It is good to be home,' he murmured under his breath.

As he walked into passport control, he caught sight of Claude leaning nonchalantly on the barrier just outside the hall. His expression of nervous apprehension was clear.

Gaston cleared customs and began walking towards him, by which time the simmering undercurrent of anger exploded like an incendiary within him.

Without a word of greeting, Gaston punched him full in the face with such a force that Claude staggered back and fell to the floor, blood pouring from his broken nose.

He gave Claude a venomous look. 'You deserved that and more for neglecting my dog,' he said.

Claude began to cry. He had nothing with which to stem the flow of blood, except the hem of his tee-shirt. He lay on the floor in the hope that Gaston would not strike him again.

Gaston stood over him hurling abuse and demanding retribution, but realised that if he lingered he might not be responsible for his actions.

As he reached out, he saw Claude cringe. 'Don't hit me, please. Let me explain.' Gaston sneered and snatched the car keys from Claude's hand, then walked off to find his car and drove out of the airport without a backward glance.

When he had gone, Claude picked himself up. He felt sick and dizzy. Someone had called the airport police, who questioned him closely. But they could not take the matter any further as Claude had lied, saying that he had merely fallen.

The officers suspected he was withholding relevant information but were forced to accept his story. They advised him to go to hospital, then departed.

Claude, fortunately, was not without funds so he took himself off to the nearest bar to recuperate and get drunk.

He tried to call Gaston several times, but the calls all went to voicemail. Finally, he texted a message saying, 'Ok, you tell me how a small dog could escape from a locked apartment.'

The combination of shock and alcohol acted like an anaesthetic to Claude's bruised body, causing him to fall asleep in the bar. Around midnight, he called a taxi and asked to be taken to central Nice.

His nose had swollen considerably but had stopped bleeding. The taxi driver dropped him off outside the hospital and refused payment for his kindness.

The hospital staff assumed that he was just another drunk who had fallen victim to his self-inflicted inebriation. The nurses patched him up and made an appointment for him to return, but he was so exhausted that he made for the beach where he slept for the remainder of the night.

It was early evening when Gaston eventually arrived home. He entered through the café, finding it in immaculate order. There was a faint odour of emulsion paint in the dining room, although the colour had not been changed. Had Giselle organised its redecoration? She had not mentioned this to him, which he thought strange.

His antique emporium had remained untouched, as the separate alarm system would admit only himself or Giselle. He went into the office and glanced at the accounts. They were all updated correctly.

The café usually closed around eight-thirty in the evening. He looked at his watch. It was only ten minutes passed eight; he thought it odd that Collette was not there clearing the tables.

The dining room looked too tidy and there was no odour of food preparation. *Perhaps she was ill*, he thought. As a result of his quick temper, he had not allowed Claude time to say or explain anything when they had met earlier at the airport, and he had been in no mood to listen either.

He looked around. Everywhere was shut up and closed off, as if the business had not continued in his absence. He was baffled. Reaching for his phone, he read Claude's message again. *Pathetic excuses,* he thought, *just trying to save his own skin, again.*

He raced up the steps to the apartment. He had not yet eaten that day, and was hungry and tired. Where was Collette?

On entering the apartment, he noticed that it had been cleaned to a near forensic standard. The furniture and ornaments had been reorganised, and it looked and smelt different. Once again he wondered if Giselle had left instructions for a deep clean in their absence, without mentioning it to him.

Then, in the air he caught a trace of Giselle's distinctive perfume. He was confused. *What is going on here?* he thought. He walked along the landing into her bedroom and was astonished to find her wardrobe doors wide open, a dress which he knew to be his wife's lying across the bed.

Just then, the bathroom door opened, and Collette appeared wearing nothing more than a small towel, her hair wet from the shower. She smiled then made a gesture with her hands, releasing the inadequate towel that had covered her body. Her invitation was unmistakable.

He stood transfixed and totally appalled. It was obvious that she had taken great advantage of their absence. Gaston felt that Giselle had been in some way defiled by Collette's blatant use of her possessions.

The woman smiled and cupped her naked breasts, offering them to him. 'Our secret,' she said.

A look of disdain crossed his features. 'You disgust me,' he snapped. 'Cover yourself and meet me in the dining room.'

He was stunned. How dare she take advantage of their absence! And as for her attempt to seduce him in such a manner? Not for one moment was he tempted to succumb to her highly questionable charms.

He slowly descended the stairs. His disbelief and acute disappointment at her shameful betrayal of their trust shocked him to his very core. Their relationship had changed irrevocably the instant he saw her in his apartment.

After he had gone, Collette sank to the floor in rage and humiliation. His look of distain and loathing had been unbearable. She had loved him since their first meeting. Keeping her feelings secret, she cherished their moments together. At times, she imagined his teasing was born out of attraction, but clearly she had been mistaken. He was just like all the other men who had passed through her life. When he married that little minx, she thought her chance had gone, until her sister had invented a cunning plan.

Gaston was still furious. He would dismiss her now on the spot, and her worthless son. Together they had overstepped the mark, and this time the situation was irretrievable.

He needed a coffee heavily laced with cognac, but searched the bar and found none. Wearily, he made his way to the cellar. As the well-oiled door swung open, he started feeling around for the elusive light switch. Sighing with exasperation, he reached further along the wall, nearly losing his step.

At that moment, he felt unseen hands on his back. The attack took just seconds, leaving him unable to retaliate as he was pushed violently down the cellar steps.

He attempted to turn mid-flight to see who had pushed him and to save himself, but as he landed he heard a sickening crack and stabs of pain captured his breath.

In a daze of pain and confusion, he heard the cellar door slam shut and the key turned. Then nothing; oblivion claimed him.

When he regained semi-consciousness, he gradually became aware of his surroundings and the pains in his body. He was lying in a pool of blood, unable to move.

The dense blackness of the cellar seemed impenetrable. A single shaft of light from a street light entered through the chink of a tiny window near the roof; night had fallen, he could see the stars through the opening. He felt for his phone but his pocket was empty. He called out in vain for help, but none came and no-one answered.

Searing pain racked his whole body. He tried to move but almost fainted with weakness. His right elbow seemed to be leaning at a strange angle. Looking down, he almost fainted when he saw the extent of his injuries – his wrist and left ankle were bleeding and swollen. He managed to staunch the flow of blood from his head wound with his other arm.

He must have passed out, as daylight was streaming through the tiny window when he awoke. His body was numb with cold, his clothing soaked in blood, and the pain in his limbs was almost unbearable. He grimaced at every movement.

Sweat trickled down his face and back, he felt faint and nauseous. The suffocating smell of dust and damp chilled his body, and he feared that he would die there in his own cellar.

With great resolve, he began to crawl towards his phone. *Please, please, don't let it be broken*, he thought desperately. 'Yes, thank God!' he cried out when he saw it was miraculously undamaged.

He rang the emergency services. When they arrived some ten minutes later, they found it necessary to remove the front door and call a locksmith; they had found the whole building locked and the alarm set.

His only thoughts were of Giselle and her reaction to his accident. She would be on her way to England by now, so he couldn't tell her – not yet. She had her own issues to resolve. He would let the doctors do their work, and perhaps his injuries would not be as incapacitating as they felt at that moment.

The ambulance jolted his body and he moaned in agony. It felt like torture. He became disoriented then sank into a stupor, but in a distant corner of his mind he could hear people shouting his name. He opened his eyes to find himself lying in a hospital bed. Tubes had been inserted into him at various points in his body, delivering blood, hydration, and pain control.

A cheerful nurse advised him of his lucky escape. If he had been detained in the cellar for another night, he would not have survived, she said with a smile. She enquired as to the cause of his accident.

'Oh, I slipped,' he said.

Although he suspected Collette of forcibly pushing him down the steps, he decided to keep his suspicions to himself for the moment, until he felt more recovered. He decided to delay any complaint to the authorities as he needed to clear his head and speak with Giselle. Fortunately, he had been given a small room of his own, which enabled him to speak to her without her hearing any background noise from the other hospital wards.

When his doctor arrived with the results of his scans, it transpired that he had broken his right elbow and wrist, while his other injuries amounted to multiple flesh wounds. He would receive a plaster cast to his arm the following day and be allowed home later that week, if the doctor was satisfied with his progress.

He tentatively rang Collette, and left a message asking her to visit him and bring his phone charger and various personal items. He was curious to gauge her reaction. *Would she dare to face him?* he wondered.

He had no pyjamas and had no intention of ever wearing any; the simple gown provided by the hospital would have to suffice. He also had no intention of staying longer that was necessary.

He surveyed his surroundings. The room was light and pleasant, and he had television and radio at his fingertips. He dreaded tasting the coffee and expected the food to be tasteless.

Checking his phone, he saw two missed calls from Giselle. He rang back, encouraging her to talk at length about events close to her heart. Feigning tiredness and hunger, he bade her goodbye then collapsed into his pillow.

He felt lightheaded as if lost in mist. When he woke some hours later, he was ravenously hungry, as he had not eaten properly for nearly two days.

His next meal would be afternoon tea, or supper as they termed it in hospital, because he had slept through lunch.

He heard his phone bleep. Collette had texted to ask if he needed any additional items. He added a small bottle of cognac, brie, and biscuits to her list.

He would be careful not to alienate her further until he had considered her motives, but she must have been his attacker. Who else could it have been? Was there someone else in the building that night?

Collette appeared later that day with his requirements. She wore a beautifully cut printed linen dress, her feet shod in cerise high-heeled sandals, her hair piled high on her head. She resembled an exotic butterfly.

She sat very close to him, occasionally touching his hand in sympathy.

He purposefully did not mention the discourse that had taken place between them in the bedroom. However, she confirmed that prior to Giselle's departure, she had given her full permission for Collette to use the apartment in their absence, as it would be company for Maude when Claude was out.

Gaston knew this was a blatant lie, as Giselle would have mentioned it to him, but he said nothing. He was in no position to argue in his present state.

Collette guessed correctly that he would be reluctant to recount their accidental meeting in her bedroom, not wishing to raise Giselle's suspicions of an illicit liaison between them.

She sat looking at him with a brazen confidence he had not previously seen in her. She made no comments regarding his accident nor enquired about his injuries.

He asked where she had visited whilst on holiday, and there was a flicker of uncertainty in her eyes before she answered. 'My parents invited me to stay for a few days,' she said.

She knew that her time off had not been authorised, which made her contradictory comment about caring for Maude sound ridiculous. She changed the subject by asking if the café was to remain open.

'Yes, naturally, but please ask before you take any leave,' he said. As Gaston looked her directly in the eye, she lowered her gaze and a slight flush illuminated her features. He regarded her suspiciously, maintaining his composure and tone of voice. He was in no position to accuse her of anything at present, but he would have her confession; he was sure of that.

When the visitors' bell sounded, she stood up, gave him a cursory glance and said she would come again the next day.

'No, you will be needed in the café,' he told her. 'Please send Claude, if he surfaces in the next few days. Needless to say, there will be much to discuss when I return home next week, and I will require a full and truthful explanation. Do you understand me, Collette?' His voice was laden with meaning.

'My only other instruction is that if Giselle calls you, she must not learn of my accident. as I will inform her in my own time, is that also understood?'

Collette lifted her head arrogantly. 'As you wish, Gaston' she replied, turned on her heel, and left him.

When a supper of vegetable soup, bread, and tart au citron arrived at five-thirty, Gaston feverishly devoured it all, including the cheese that Collette had brought him together with most of the small bottle of cognac.

A period of about twenty minutes passed, when a wrenching pain took hold of his stomach. He could barely breathe, perspiration covered his entire body, and his vision had blurred.

He rang for the nurse, who came just as he was violently ill all over the floor. His torture continued all night and into the next day, leaving him sore, lethargic, and disconsolate.

He was terrified that Giselle would ring him, as he would no longer be able to conceal his illness. He sent her frequent inconsequential texts to keep her happy.

The medical staff were unimpressed when they learned that he had imbibed alcohol on hospital premises. He was severely reprimanded by his doctor, who asked to be given the remainder of the bottle.

Gaston endured yet another night of pain as he had not taken the drugs prescribed for him. He became irritable and fractious whilst waiting for his cast to be applied. Such was his annoyance that he made the decision to discharge himself the following day.

By lunchtime, the wait had become interminable. Then the doctor appeared looking rather serious. 'Gaston, we have received the laboratory results of your unfortunate gastric incident. It would appear that you have been poisoned; the brandy contained traces of belladonna. I am sorry, but I must inform the gendarmerie.'

In a flash of realisation, Gaston reached for his phone and rang the vet in Honfleur to ask if he had kept a record of the type of poison which killed Maude.

The vet confirmed immediately that the sweet but deadly poison was indeed belladonna. The dog could easily have eaten the berries whilst on a walk in the woods with Claude. Had her body not been deposited on Inez's doorstep, her death might have been considered as just an unfortunate accident.

Gaston was tormented by the thought that Collette may have an accomplice. He did not want to believe that Claude was involved in attempted murder.

If his detention in Menton was deliberate, then Giselle might also be in danger. He felt powerless and at a loss as to the motive.

He fell back onto his pillows, his mind in turmoil, his body weak. The effects of the poison would take a few days to subside. When lunchtime came, he was unable to drink even a little soup.

Later that afternoon, a gendarme appeared to take a statement. This took much longer than anticipated, as Gaston was forced to include Maude's death and the attack in Paris to his list of complaints.

Paris, Honfleur, and now Menton. How low would this conspiracy sink? Was it now at an end? His mind overflowed with questions, but no answers.

He was becoming more and more convinced that Collette had orchestrated all three incidents. *But what was her motive?* he asked himself. *I am not a wealthy man. Was revenge her motive for his attack on her son at the airport? No*, he thought, *there is more to be discovered.* He was thankful that the gendarmes would be continuing the investigation, as he felt depleted and nonplussed.

When the gendarme had departed, Gaston rang Collette and ordered her without explanation to close the shop immediately. He then rang Claude to enquire of his whereabouts, asking if he would visit him in hospital or risk losing his job.

But Claude advised him to park his job in the shade of his underpants, and abruptly ended the call.

Immediately, Gaston rang a locksmith and asked him to visit Café Villande and to change every lock on the premises, then to deliver the new keys to him in hospital.

I must make sure that evil witch is never in a position to harm anyone ever again, he thought to himself. *How could he have been so trusting and gullible?* He felt duped and embarrassed. He was so tempted to ring Giselle and ask her to fly home, as he needed her now more than ever.

He was just reaching for his phone to ring her when the cheerful nurse reappeared to administer his pain control. He asked her if she knew of anyone who would act as a temporary cook/housekeeper, as he was expecting to be discharged at the end of the week. The nurse smiled broadly and said that she would be happy to help.

Panic seized him. She was very young, newly qualified, and rather pretty. He imagined a more mature lady would have been more suitable.

He respectfully refused her kind offer, explaining that he would be in enough hot water when Giselle heard of his recent difficulties, but if she knew there was a pretty girl in attendance she would be seriously upset that he had not confided in her earlier.

The nurse suggested that her mother might be a safe choice. She had cared for her father until his untimely death, and was also an accomplished cook.

He agreed to meet the woman, hoping that the nurse had inherited her looks from her father.

The antiseptic smell of the hospital made him feel queasy, and the constant noise made by his fellow patients and nursing staff carrying out their duties kept him awake at night. And he hated being captive and shut away from the beach.

In his wakeful dark hours of the night, he mused about his childhood.

He was an only child, born of two academics. They had met whilst studying for their law degrees at home in Paris.

His mother – a tall, slim woman now in her seventy-fifth year – had a ramrod straight deportment. She held a preference for wearing long cardigans with pockets to carry her various personal possessions, as she disliked handbags. She remained all of her life a reticent swot.

She'd never had any intention to marry, as she considered children to be a time-consuming abomination and never quite knew what to expect from them. She also abhorred illness of any kind, which is the reason he had not contacted her to tell of his accident.

His father was an introspective barrister who specialised in the criminal courts. His wife thought he preferred the company of murders to her own.

A quiet man, short of stature, he would go unnoticed in any group of people. However, his mind was as cunning as a fox hunting its prey.

When Gaston's mother became pregnant, she had decided a move to the coast would be a more convivial place to raise a child. Properties would be less expensive and staff, particularly nannies, would be easier to hire.

They purchased a house near the beach and gave it their surname, Villande.

Initially, the accommodation had been unsuitable for their needs, so an architect was engaged to redesign the building, giving them separate offices on the ground floor, and leaving the upper floor to convert into an apartment.

When they grew tired of the provinces and returned to Paris, they had part of the ground floor converted to a café for Gaston to manage in their absence, as he had no inclination to be either a lawyer or to live in the capital.

He woke suddenly, the intense sunlight of the Cote d'Azur streaming through the window. Had he dreamt or mused all night?

The cheerful nurse came in and checked his blood pressure, and asked why his wife had not visited him. He explained that she was abroad attending to family issues, and that he would be joining her in a few days' time.

She was surprised. 'Please, Gaston,' she said, 'do not over-exert yourself or you will be back with us again.' She smiled sweetly then left him to his interminably boring day.

After a breakfast of fruit and coffee, he decided to loosen his body by resuming his daily yoga practice which, apart from a few stretches had become minimal or non-existent, and he was too restless to read.

He rang Giselle to offer a part confession, so as to lessen the initial shock of her seeing the extent of his injuries. He looked as though he had just returned from a war zone. *Hmm,* he thought, *I have been through the wars of late. However, the situation is about to change.*

Gaston's mood improved after he had managed to retain a supper of scrambled eggs on brioche toast. He rang Giselle again that evening and gave her the welcome news that he was determined to travel to England in the next few days.

He reassured her that he was being well looked after and that his injuries amounted to no more than a few scratches.

The following morning, after a sound night's sleep, he received a visit from the gendarme looking after his case. He informed Gaston that Collette had been charged and taken into custody, pending further investigations into the previous incidents in Paris and Menton. Her lawyer had applied for bail, but it had been refused.

The mystery, he thought with some relief, *was almost solved. Justice would be served, but the motive still remained elusive.* Gaston would leave no stone unturned in his quest to extract his revenge on Collette and any of her associates who had been complicit in Maude's murder.

He was discharged a few days later with his arm in plaster, but life at home was difficult for an active man left alone with a temporary disability. With the café closed, he relied on takeaway meals and box-sets for company as he did not wish to be questioned, stared at, or pitied by his friends and neighbours.

Giselle rang to wish him *bon voyage* and enquired after his health and temper. He managed the whole conversation with evasive answers to her questions, and felt satisfied and not a little smug with his verbal deceptions. But he knew full well that he would pay for them later.

The day prior to his departure, he visited the gendarmerie and asked to speak with Collette. Permission was granted on condition that a gendarme be present.

He was advised to be brief and concise, and was then called to a side cubicle near the visiting room. Collette was seated very upright with her hands folded.

She was wearing a blue cotton dress that resembled a prison uniform.

He had never seen her without the benefit of make-up before. Nevertheless, her defiant expression and unwavering stare told him that she was not going to surrender her dignity under any circumstances.

Gaston looked steadily into her face and asked her to explain why she had murdered Maude and attempted to poison him. 'Who was your accomplice?' he asked. 'What have I ever done to incur your wrath? Why did you have to poison a defenceless animal? Tell me, Collette, why?'

Collette turned on him with a vicious sneer. 'You will know soon enough,' she said. Her threat was clear, and implied that her accomplice was still out there, waiting for another opportunity to strike. Then she stood up, turned on her heel, and demanded to be taken from the room.

Gaston thanked the gendarmerie and called a taxi to take him home.

Enraged by Collette's refusal to elaborate further, he was loath to admit that she had unnerved him. *Thankfully, Giselle was safe in England and away from this mess,* he thought.

When he arrived home, he checked every room, including the professionally cleaned cellar, viewing it from the comparative safety of the top step. A shiver of fear ran down his spine. *I am not going down there yet,* he said to himself.

He needed fresh air and a decent meal, so he left the house, checking and re-checking the lock. *Am I becoming paranoid?* he thought.

It was early evening. The restaurants close to the beach were preparing for early evening diners such as himself, waiters were changing the daytime tablecloths to the starched white variety for the evening crowd, and candles and flowers were being placed on the tables to create a romantic atmosphere. He thought wistfully of Giselle. So intense was his longing for her that he could not face sitting alone in a restaurant, so he bought yet another takeaway meal and proceeded to have a lonely picnic on the beach.

He rang Claude's number again. This time, to his surprise, he heard an international ring tone. *Well, no surprise there,* he thought. *He has bolted to avoid arrest, and left his own mother to be his scapegoat.*

As Gaston sat on the beach just yards from his home, his thoughts turned to little Maud. *She must have suffered,* he thought. *Being poisoned is a painful experience, and I should know.* He sat for a while trying to read a book as the gentle waves lapped the shore. Their lonely apartment would fail again that evening to offer any comfort and solace; he felt like a small boat cast adrift in a huge ocean of uncertainty. He stood up and started walking towards home, feeling dejected and very sorry for himself.

He turned before entering the apartment and looked back down the beach, half expecting to see his dog rushing towards him, barking her demands as usual.

The memory pierced him with a spear of such deep sorrow that he was thankful for the dusk, as his silent tears soon turned to heart-rending sobs.

Gaston's injuries were taking longer to heal than he had anticipated. The bruising to his face made him look like a boxer who had lost the fight, he was still limping like an invalid, and his plastered arm inhibited him to such an extent that he felt like screaming. *Fine, ok,* he thought, remonstrating with himself. *Get a grip and stop being pathetic.*

Two days of pure indolence and reflection followed while he rested, took salt baths three times daily, read anything and everything, listened to music, watched television, and meditated. 'Healer heal thyself' was his constant mantra.

When Giselle rang him the following afternoon, for the first time in days he agreed to share Facetime with her. When she saw her poor wounded husband, she just wept. He had expected an entirely different reaction; in some ways, her temper was easier to deal with than her tears.

Gaston carefully explained everything, his distasteful encounters with Collette, and his extended stay in hospital due to her secret administration of belladonna.

Giselle was appalled at Gaston's revelations. She would have rushed to his side had she known the extent of his injuries, but it would have meant leaving Inez without her support in the bosom of hostility that was her former home.

He confessed to feeling the strain of having to conceal his true condition, evading her questions in order not to cause her concern when he was perfectly capable of fending for himself. When their call ended, he sighed with relief, and Immediately went online to buy his travel tickets from Nice to London, then onward to Newcastle International, where Giselle would be waiting for him.

Part Six
Roxberg Gate

On a day like any other, Giselle and her mother interspersed their time discussing their life's mysteries and dilemmas and, if any, regrets.

'A human life is built of many layers, some smooth, others not so. As life moves forward, its challenges and disappointments must be conquered,' said Inez. This they had to accept with good grace and fortitude.

They both missed Gaston terribly. He exuded a masculine strength that could be relied on in an emergency, and they both felt secure and protected in his company. They also missed his cryptic sense of humour that made them laugh in difficult times.

His unplanned departure and subsequent accident in Menton had constituted a huge setback to their plan. Their concern for his health had delayed their travel for England, as Giselle had refused to leave France until she received the assurance that he was recovering well.

With their heavy suitcases packed and a taxi waiting to take them to Le Havre, it was with some trepidation that they finally began their journey. Giselle's nails were bitten to the quick with worry, but Gaston was adamant that she should not change her plans to journey to England in all haste.

Inez was loath to admit even to herself the nervous disquiet she felt at the thought of meeting her mercurial husband once more, as beneath his suave exterior lay a cruel and devious infidel.

The weather that morning had an unusually crisp autumnal air. 'We had better get used to this chilly weather,' said Inez, smiling at her daughter. They were warmly dressed in layers of cashmere.

'Anyone would think we are visiting the Arctic,' said Giselle, and they both laughed.

'Trust me,' said Inez, 'we might as well be.'

They wrapped their scarves neatly into their necks, snuggled themselves deeper into their coats, and set off for the sometimes inhospitable northern English coast, like intrepid explorers.

Their flight connections proceeded smoothly and without delay. From the air they could see the verdant green landscape shrouded in fine drizzle. They looked at each other and grimaced.

On arrival at the airport, they collected a hire car. 'I will drive,' said Giselle, setting the sat-nav. 'I am surprised that damp pile of ancient stone even has a postcode,' she laughed.

Then she remembered that they were staying at a hotel in a nearby village for a couple of nights. The journey was fraught as she kept forgetting to drive on the left, almost giving her mother a seizure.

They were both physically and mentally exhausted by the time they eventually arrived at the hotel. It was late afternoon, dusk had fallen, and they were in need of high tea or an early dinner and a cognac to warm them.

The quaint family-run hotel looked exactly as Inez had remembered. Virginia creeper clothed the walls, their burnished leaves falling like darts of fire.

A warm welcome awaited them, and the manager remembered Inez from years before when she had been the chatelaine in residence at Roxberg Gate.

They sank into deep armchairs arranged around a blazing log fire and ordered reviving pots of tea and home-made scones.

'Our unpacking can wait,' said Inez, as she saw their luggage disappear upstairs in the strong arms of the manager's son.

They lingered over tea, savouring their well-earned indolence, and Inez invited the manager to join them in a brandy. When the woman accepted and made herself comfortable, Inez asked quite blatantly if she would be happy to share any interesting pieces of gossip regarding her husband or his mistress.

The manager confided that their butler was the only person from the lodge to step inside her establishment. 'Being Austrian,' she explained, 'he likes a pint or two of lager.' On occasions, it seemed, the man would drink too much then express his dislike of the late evening deliveries to the house, by either land or sea, which he was expected to receive. 'He never mentioned anyone else. More than his job's worth,' the manager said.

Giselle, embarrassed by her mother's forthright questioning, decided to shower before dinner and ring Gaston. She arranged to meet Inez in the dining room later that evening.

The décor and furniture in her bedroom was more than adequate for a short stay. A large chest of drawers stood under the window, waiting to receive their newly-purchased thermals and woollies. Chintzy curtains and bedcovers lent a cosy air of familiarity and comfort.

Giselle sighed when she saw the large double bed, as she longed to hold her husband in her arms.

Showered and dressed, mother and daughter went directly into the crowded dining room and were shown to a discreet table in an alcove away from the other diners, so their conversation could not be overheard.

As they perused the menu, they noticed other diners giving them speculative glances. They ignored this superficial attention and conducted their entire conversation in French, discussing at length and in great detail their fears, real or imagined. They both confessed the deep misgivings they harboured regarding their visit to the lodge, which was planned for the next day.

After a good night's sleep, with only the sounds of the country to wake them, they rose early and were up and dressed as the delicious smell of breakfast permeated from the kitchen into their rooms, making them feel ravenous. They ate locally-sourced bacon, eggs, and home-baked bread smeared with rich butter and fragrant honey. The hotel manager and her staff extended such a warm welcome that Giselle told her mother she would stay there for the duration of the visit, if her father's welcome proved to be lukewarm.

The other members of staff who lived in the village and had heard the story of Inez's reluctant departure some years earlier, were intrigued by her reappearance.

Unlike their manager, they twittered gossip like finches around a bird table, telling Inez that the staff employed at the lodge lived within its walls, they were all foreign, neither news nor rumour ever escaped its portals, and that visitors in large vehicles were often seen disappearing through the gates. Apparently, their visits were short-lived, raising suspicious comments among the villagers.

They all agreed that the Roxberg Gate estate must be thriving, but were not sure which line of business provided the funds for the extensive renovations which had been carried out on the Lodge in recent years. The sophisticated security system protected the privacy of its occupants, but the often-seen prying eye of a telephoto lens or drone could not.

Giselle grew impatient with the gossiping staff. She disapproved of their candour and demanded to leave; as usual, she had her way. She virtually ran up the stairs, talking under her breath, her temper rising.

'Mother, do hurry. We have waited for years to see Honoré, don't delay with idle chatter.' Then, filled with abject remorse, she apologised and gave her mother a hug.

Inez reached for her phone and rang Henry's landline. Margot answered the call, her tight-lipped voice no more welcoming than a cold shower.

She informed Inez that Henry was out on estate business and was not expected back until late afternoon. Inez stood for a moment rooted to the spot with incandescent rage. After some moments, she took a deep breath.

"Why is he not at home to greet us?' she said. 'He knew that we were visiting today. You may expect us at eleven-thirty this morning, and I must insist on seeing my daughter.'

Margot acquiesced. 'As you wish,' she replied. A click, and the line was dead.

Inez turned to Giselle in an absolute fury. 'I fear we are facing an uphill struggle, my darling, but this time

I will not be deterred. It is time I discovered the hold she has over my husband.'

They set off in pouring rain, this time with Inez at the wheel, and drove in the direction of the Lodge. As the turreted building came into view, they were faced with large and imposing, closed outer entrance gates, held in place at each side by tall stone pillars, topped with stone eagles standing sentinel over them.

Giselle pressed the intercom button to announce their arrival. It was some five minutes before the gates slowly began to open, then closed behind them.

Two large dogs leapt forward baring their teeth. They rushed at the car, scraping at the door, which unnerved Inez as she was concerned that she might accidentally injure one of them. She drove on under a second portcullis gate and into an enclosed courtyard.

A blustery sea breeze caught their breath as they stepped from the car. Looking upwards, they saw and heard sea birds screaming their reproach above their heads. Inez's eye was caught by a figure standing watching them from a turret window which overlooked the courtyard. Giselle looked at her mother but did not see the figure.

'The harbingers of bad luck, perhaps,' she smiled ruefully, folding her coat tighter around her.

Max, Henry's servile butler, was waiting at the heavy oak entrance door to greet them. He smiled, bowing slightly. 'Good morning, Madame Roxberg,' he said, then bowed slightly in Giselle's direction. 'Madame Villande. It is my pleasure to see you both again.

He looked distinctly uncomfortable and kept his head lowered, as he knew the security cameras would be focused in their direction and they would be subject to Margot's scrutiny.

He invited them to follow him inside, and a shiver of apprehension passed through Giselle's body as she surveyed her birthplace. *It resembles a prison,* she thought, looking up at the battlements. The turrets looked more forbidding than she remembered, and the grounds were stark, with no flower borders or ornaments to relieve the austerity of the granite stone walls.

The hall also was not as she had remembered it, baronial in style but somehow more elegant and in a good state of repair. The carved hammer beam ceiling had been restored to its former glory, the walls decorated in a mural scene of the Belvedere gardens in Vienna. A Chinese silk rug almost completely covered the entire hall floor.

Inez was astounded at the sumptuous furnishings. *Henry's business interests have proved lucrative,* she thought. There was a large medieval oak table in the centre of the hall. Standing at its centre, sending their all-pervading sickly scent, was a vase of Michaelmas daisies.

So, thought Inez, *the tyranny has begun.* Margot's message was clear. She had remembered that this was the scent Inez found unbearably repellent; it had made her violently nauseous when pregnant with Honoré. Inez put her handkerchief over her face and hurried into the morning room. Giselle followed, perplexed at her mother's rapid escape.

Inez turned to her daughter. 'It has started,' she said. 'She meant to upset me from the outset.'

Max returned with a glass of water for Inez, and said that coffee and biscuits would follow shortly.

The windows of her favourite room overlooked the gardens that ran, unfenced, down to the cliffs and on to a tiny spit of a beach. Looking up, she noted the intricate plasterwork ceiling had been painted in a lime wash. A large, white Italian marble fireplace stood at the far end; the pale celandine coloured silk furnishings were of her own choosing. The room was a shrine to happier days before the taint of infidelity destroyed her marriage.

This was the room which Inez had used as her studio in the early years of her marriage to Henry. It imbued her with a sudden feeling of sadness and of the husband she lost. *Was he ever mine?* she thought.

The two women exchanged conspiratorial looks but said nothing. Max returned bearing a silver tray with the requisite coffee and biscuits, with linen napkins provided for their use.

He said Miss Honoré was resting and would be pleased to receive them for a short time within the hour, then he bowed and withdrew.

By this time, Inez was nearly beside herself with impatience. 'I have a good mind to take our coffee upstairs and insist we see her,' she said.

Giselle tried to calm her, 'Mother, please hold your temper. We don't even know where she is, and your being difficult will not benefit our cause.'

Columns of steam rose from the coffee pot rose like clouds on a winter's day.

The unheated room was icy cold, but a fire had been prepared with twigs and newspaper rolled into balls, and the scuttle was full of coal and logs. Giselle hunted for matches and found them behind the clock on the chimney piece.

In no time at all she had a roaring blaze to warm them. As she repositioned the fire guard, with her back to the door, she heard the turn of the door handle and saw her mother lift her chin and narrow her eyes. She hardly recognised the expression registered on her mother's beautiful features.

Inez's look of thinly-veiled distaste was directed at the woman now entering the room. Medusa herself could not have instilled more terror in her victims.

Margot had made her entrance. Her perfume filled the room, her svelte body encased in a long sleeved, closely-fitting dress the colour of midnight blue. A shawl was thrown casually around her shoulders, and her dark hair was long and lustrous, caught in a knot to the side of her long, creamy neck.

If Giselle and Inez had imagined meeting a time-worn housekeeper, they could not have been more mistaken. The woman standing before them represented good taste personified.

Inez and Margot appraised each other with expressions of malevolent dislike.

Margot offered no polite greeting or platitude. 'Honoré will see you now. I trust your visit will be short, as she tires easily. Please follow me.'

Reading her mother's thoughts, Giselle prepared herself for an explosion of temper, but Inez remained tight-lipped.

Giselle stepped forward, her face very close to Margot's. In a low voice laden with meaning, she said, 'I am a daughter of this house, and I will see my sister in my own time. Where is she to be found?'

'As you wish,' replied Margot. 'She occupies The Vienna Suite.'

Giselle continued haughtily, 'We will be a party of three when my husband joins us for an indefinite period at the end of this week. Please have our rooms ready by tomorrow.'

Margot inclined her head and silently left the room. Immediately, Inez rushed to open a window to eliminate the scent of her perfume.

When they had finished their coffee, they decided to look for Honoré. Just then, Max came in to collect the tray.

'Thank you, Max. Perhaps you would be kind enough to lead us to Honoré's suite,' said Inez.

He led them through the hall and up the staircase leading to the south wing.

They were both surprised, as this part of the lodge had always been unused when Inez had been in residence.

The rooms, which benefited from the warmth of the sun, had been used exclusively by Henry's parents when they were alive, hence the need for some extensive updating and repairs. Inez looked around at the transformation which had occurred since her departure.

As they walked along the hallway, they marvelled at the expensive furnishings. It became increasingly obvious that a considerable amount of money had been spent in making the rooms extremely luxurious.

Inez turned to the butler. 'Max, we will be staying here from tomorrow and would prefer our rooms to be in this wing, please.'

He bowed. 'As you wish, madame. I will give your instructions to the housekeeping staff, ' he replied stiffly.

At the end of a long corridor, a door came into view. The sign read: *The Vienna Suite, please knock before entering.*

As requested, they tapped the door and held their breath in trepidation; neither of them had seen Honoré for almost five years. A listless voice bade them enter.

She was sitting in a wheelchair facing large, double height window, her face turned away from them. Without turning, she asked them to sit on a sofa at the side of the room.

Inez rushed towards her. 'My darling, let me embrace you. It has been so long since we have been allowed to visit you.'

Honoré looked downcast. 'l am no longer the daughter you knew,' she said. 'My injuries have deprived me of a normal life. I have nothing to live for.' She turned slowly to look at them.

The face held in their memories bore almost no resemblance to the face before them. The young woman's features had altered irrevocably; even the tone of her voice had changed.

Inez longed to throw her arms around her daughter, to offer reassurance and expressions of love, but Giselle cautioned her mother.

'Please be patient, Mother. Reminiscing can be a painful experience for us all.

Giselle asked her sister how she spent her time and if she felt able to travel.

Honoré explained that she had learned the German language of their father, and spent her time as a translator of documents. She no longer travelled beyond the estate boundaries, however, as her infirmities imposed constant pain upon her.

Honoré, in turn, asked Giselle about her life with Gaston – the man she had secretly fallen in love with, as did Giselle.

As the morning deepened into the late afternoon, they had become so lost in conversation they had failed to notice that lunchtime had come and gone.

When Inez tentatively broached the subject of Honoré's accident, her face changed, like a grotesque mask distorting her countenance.

She complained of fatigue and turned away from them. 'Please leave,' she said tersely. 'You ask too many questions.' They apologised, promising to return the following day.

Hearing voices, they hurried downstairs. To their dismay, the conversation was being conducted entirely in German. Mother and daughter looked at each other askance, as neither spoke or understood a word of the language.

Henry had returned from his business appointments. He looked pleasantly surprised to see them both, as Margot had informed him they would not be arriving until the following day.

Giselle gave him a long hug and said how much she had missed him.

Henry looked over her head at Inez. *She still has her aura*, he thought, as his eyes noted every curve of her body. *She has an undefinable presence of latent cosmopolitan sexuality.* He felt his senses stir. *She would never know*, he thought. *If she knew the absolute truth, he would lose her forever.*

As their eyes met, Inez defiantly held his appraising stare. Her mind flooded with half-forgotten emotions of rejection and disappointment.

Henry was glad they had not completely severed their connection to each other.

Distant friends – that was the deal her father had imposed on him after the children came along. In return, Henry would receive an agreed monthly sum of money to stay out of her life.

On the death of her father, a large final payment would be made to him and a solemn promise extracted. But as he looked at his estranged wife, he doubted he would be able to keep his promise.

Inez's father had heard rumours that Henry's father, and later Henry himself, had in some way been complicit in dealing with art treasures confiscated by the Nazi Party during the Second World War. The evidence against them had been submitted by reliable sources but had never been substantiated. However, dark rumours persisted.

There was no sign of illness in Henry's handsome face. His posture remained dignified and his waistline trim.

He smiled broadly at her. 'How well you look, Inez. I am honoured by your visit. Perhaps you would indulge me further by staying to dinner this evening? I have business in Vienna for a few days from tomorrow, and I would like to spend time with you both.'

Inez smiled, giving him a long look of oblique suspicion, but Giselle answered for them both by immediately accepting her father's invitation.

As she walked towards the morning room to retrieve her handbag, Inez turned to look back at her mercurial husband. An unwelcome rush of emotion engulfed her; she was still in love with him. She hid her confusion and hoped that he had not noticed the flush on her cheeks. *Could I recapture this man?* she wondered with a sigh. *But then, was he ever truly mine?*

When Henry moved slightly, she saw a shadowy figure in the corner of the room.

Margot, her adversary, had entered silently, her sombre presence changing their light-hearted mood.

Inez wondered how long she had been standing watching them.

Giselle and Inez were disconcerted to hear that all conversations around the house were still being conducted entirely in German. This would be a distinct disadvantage to any thought of subterfuge or just plain eavesdropping.

Inez had taken a course in her husband's native language when first married, but had lapsed when the pair went their separate ways.

Having accepted Henry's invitation to dine, the women decided to use the intervening two hours before dinner to explore the house. Inez made her way to the study, where she tentatively tapped the door then looked in.

She found Henry sitting at his desk, head lowered, deep in thought. For a moment she thought him asleep, but he turned and looked into her eyes, his expression serious and unsmiling.

He invited her to sit beside him on a sofa, a fire smouldering in the hearth. They engaged in superficial conversation that almost anyone would hold with a stranger at a train station. As her words trailed into silence, she found courage to ask him a favour.

'Henry, I would like us to talk somewhere, anywhere, away from this place. Not now or tomorrow, but some time in the future. I need to make sense of the years we spent together.'

He took her hand and looked sadly into her eyes. 'Yes, my love, but not yet,' he replied.

She resigned herself to his wishes, hiding her disappointment. He had crossed an indefinable boundary long ago, one which she herself found impossible to navigate.

In exasperation, she abruptly left the room and caught Margot outside the door. She had obviously been listening to their conversation, but her expression was inscrutable and she seemed unconcerned at being caught flagrantly eavesdropping.

She surveyed Inez with a degree of hauteur. 'I have prepared rooms for you and your daughter,' she said, then paused and looked steadily into Inez's upturned face. 'How fortunate you are to have two daughters still living. As you are aware, I lost Simone when your Honoré was rescued. But heed my warning, I will not lose Henry.'

Her slender fingers flexed and twitched as she spoke, and there was something in her look that sent writhing tendrils of fear through Inez's body.

She said nothing and moved forward, but Margot side-stepped into her path, preventing her from leaving. The housekeeper's eyes were wide and staring, her fingers constantly flexing as if enacting strangulation; her hypnotic stare held years of embittered jealous hatred.

Anger and indignation swelled inside Inez, crystallising her emotions and focusing her mind. 'Margot,' she said calmly, 'I will never draw a veil over the past and I intend to expose the fissures in your devious character. I am and always will be Henry's wife, and may I also remind you that he chose me whilst you were under his roof.'

As Margot stalked off, Inez realised at that moment that there would be no retreat. She wanted her life back, the life that she had allowed Margot to steal from her so many years ago.

Just then she heard Giselle calling her. 'Mother, where are you? Oh, there you are.' She stopped wearily when she saw her mother's face.

When Inez recounted her skirmish with Margot, Giselle began to wonder if they had made a mistake in visiting their family. Surely together they could out-manoeuvre Margot? She would speak with her father when a suitable opportunity presented itself. In the meantime, Gaston had rung and confessed to more of his injuries, but said that he would explain fully when they met at the weekend.

Just then, they heard the sound of an engine. Were more visitors expected today? A large, black, unnamed commercial vehicle with a foreign registration plate made its way to the rear door where the kitchens were situated. Giselle and Inez kept watch from the dining room window and after a few minutes it departed. A delivery of some sort, perhaps? They thought no more of it.

They decided to visit Honoré to ask if she intended to come downstairs to dine that evening. Henry had installed a lift in her suite after her accident, enabling her easy access to the main rooms of the lodge without hindrance.

They tapped her door and looked in without waiting for a response. To their amazement, they found her sitting in a comfortable armchair enjoying the view from her large bay window. She and Margot were laughing and holding hands, the remnants of afternoon tea lay between them, the fading early afternoon light from the casement falling directly onto their faces.

Inez asked if she and Giselle could speak to Honoré in private. Honoré shrugged and looked to Margot for her approval. Margot's face froze into a mask of disdain, but she stood up and removed the tray.

She looked directly at Giselle. 'Your sister tires easily. Do not to distress her with more unnecessary questions, she has suffered from an impaired memory since her accident.' With that, she left, leaving the door ajar.

Suspecting that Margot would listen to their conversation, Inez closed the door with a firm, decisive click

They quietly advanced toward Honoré. She was looking vaguely out of the window to the garden where her close friend Flora, the young estate gardener, was planting bulbs for her to enjoy the following spring. She loved to choose the planting schemes for the flower and vegetable gardens.

Flora had become her constant companion during the late spring and summer months when Honoré felt able to sit outdoors and discuss the merits or disadvantages of each plant.

During the dark and gloomy winter period when tempestuous gales and mountainous seas lashed the embrasures of the north wing, they would sit at the windows and watch Mother Nature unleash her fury, or play board games and cards in the warmth and comfort of the Vienna Suite.

Flora herself was like a sunflower head, always smiling and ready to play or read to Honoré when depression and self-pity held her in its grasp.

Giselle knelt at Honoré's feet and took her hand. 'My darling sister, I have missed you so much. Our parents' difficulties are not ours to bear. Please take time to consider how I might contribute to your happiness. My only wish is to help you. Perhaps if you spent the winter months with us, we would lift your spirits?' she suggested.

Honoré turned to look at her sister, her face scarred and distorted. The operations to restore any resemblance of her former appearance had failed, and she had become a stranger both in looks and manner. The very thought of allowing Gaston of all people to see her face filled Honoré with dread. She would refuse to see him and keep to her room when he arrived for the weekend.

They sat for a while discussing Giselle's life since her marriage. Inez quietly listened to their easy discourse, keeping her distance so as not to interrupt their sisterly chatter.

As she watched them affectionately, she noticed Honoré nervously clenching and flexing her fingers, her unconscious movements similar to those of Margot's. Insidious tentacles of doubt began to creep into Inez's mind.

In her mother's absence, Honoré would have looked to Margot, as any child would look to its mother. *It is only natural that she has adopted her mannerisms*, she thought.

Inez scrutinised the girl's face, hoping to recognise in her something of herself. *Is this my daughter?* she wondered. *Is this really Honoré?* The alterations in her appearance, character, and even her voice – she had now acquired a German accent – had all been attributed to her accident.

Shameful feelings of guilt flooded through Inez. She should have been here to care for her daughter; she should have taken Henry to court in order to gain access and insisted on being part of her recovery team.

Why had she been prevented from visiting Honoré when the girl most needed her mother?

Her mind was filled with tormented thoughts and unanswered questions. *Where lies the truth of what really happened on that fateful mountain in Austria?* she thought. *If only I had been here when she returned, a different course of action might have been taken.* If there had been foul play of some kind, she would have exposed it. Inez continued to sit and torment herself whilst watching her daughters. She sighed. She had so many regrets that could never be reconciled, both physically and emotionally.

Inez thought her suspicions too dreadful to contemplate. For the moment, she must conceal her fears even from Giselle. If this young woman was not her child, then who was the poor abandoned soul lying in the unkempt family churchyard?

There was a tap at the door. Max excused himself and said that a buffet lunch had been prepared and was awaiting them in the dining room.

Giselle asked Honoré if they could continue their conversation downstairs after lunch, but Honoré feigned tiredness, saying that she would join them that evening.

During lunch, Inez conducted a cerebral debate with herself with regard to Honoré's true identity; disturbing feelings continued to shape her thoughts that afternoon. Her fears, rational or irrational, were something she felt could only be discussed with Gaston. She valued his opinions; he would make sense of her theories.

In the meantime, she would keep her suspicions hidden and remain discreetly watchful.

After lunch, the weather brightened, clouds sent scudding across the pale grey sky by a brisk northerly breeze. They dressed warmly then descended to the boot room in search of suitable footwear for their muddy outdoor expedition.

Giselle had seen the spit of a beach from an upstairs window and was keen to explore the seaward side of the lodge.

As they were walking across the courtyard searching for an open door out onto the rocky outcrop which led to the beach and its jetty, they heard someone calling.

Max came running toward them. 'Madame, where are you going? Unaccompanied walks can be dangerous in this vicinity,' he said.

'But I am not alone,' she replied. 'I have my daughter for company and our phones to call for help. Please don't fuss. We need fresh air, and we are accustomed to the sea and coast.'

Max looked doubtful and kept turning to look at the lodge, as if seeking advice as how to proceed. His saturnine face revealed nothing of his inner panic.

'I will lock the dogs up for one hour,' he replied. 'With the greatest respect, madame, please speak to me before deciding to venture out again.'

When he had gone, Giselle pouted. 'Cheek!' she expostulated. 'Pompous little man.'

'No, my dear,' said her mother. 'He looked frightened. Something is wrong here, I sense it. We must be very careful until Gaston arrives.'

They turned, retraced their steps, and made instead for the walled garden. They called to Flora as she weeded around her newly-planted sprout plants, then they walked onward and beyond into the private churchyard belonging to the lodge.

The tiny gothic church was bathed in the weak and dying afternoon sun.

Masses of yellow and blue autumn crocus had peeped through the algae and carpeted the ground around the porch, alleviating the sombre atmosphere of death and decay.

They tried the door but found it locked. 'I wonder if Simone is buried in the family vault,' said Giselle, rattling the door lock. Looking around they decided to carry out a meticulous search of the churchyard. By this time, nearly an hour had passed.

'Surely Max wouldn't let the dogs out until we are safe indoors,' said Inez, looking at Giselle for her agreement.

Inez, her eye drawn to the furthest part of the tiny graveyard, felt a strange compulsion to investigate further. They walked through pools of mud and stinging nettles to discover a wretched little grave, isolated from the others, and situated in a dark corner under a huge pine tree.

Moss and algae covered its surface, perennial weeds suffocating the surrounding earth. 'No-one has been here for years,' observed Giselle sadly.

A still, stagnant, all-pervading air of deep melancholy invaded them as they looked with conflicting emotions upon Simone's last resting place.

'Mother, I know this difficult for you to accept, but she was my half-sister, and I loved her equally as much as Honoré,' she said.

It was inconceivable, thought Inez, *that Margot would allow her daughter's remains to be cast out into such a miserable place.* The small semi-circular rustic stone simply read 'Simone, died 2010, Age 19 years.'

They saw no empty vessel to hold a flower of fond remembrance, no written verse of love for one so precious.

At that moment, a light breeze wove pine-scented air through the branches overhead. *It's not me*, it seemed to whisper. *I am not Simone.*

Tears welled and began streaming down Giselle's beautiful face. Her mind filled with unspoken grief and regret at not seeing more of Honoré prior to her accident. She began to shiver uncontrollably, her heart beating fast in her breast.

"Mother, I feel an entity within me. She is here. My sister… not Simone.'

She looked in desperation around the churchyard for the ghost of her long dead sister.

Taking Inez's hand, she pulled her away from the grave. 'The devil is here in this place,' Giselle said, her voice shrill and frightened.

Inez took one last look at the headstone, the weight of misery upon her as they hurried away.

Giselle implored her mother, 'Let's return to the hotel tonight, please. We need to rest, clear our minds, and restore our strength. We can return tomorrow and wait for Gaston, then stay until our concerns have been resolved.'

'My darling, calm yourself. We have been invited and must stay. I want to avoid any conflict that may damage our quest for truth. It will be interesting to see for ourselves how their lives have changed since our departure'.

A lingering sense of pathos clouded their minds as, with linked arms, they retraced their steps. By now, the sun had almost gone and been replaced by spots of rain.

As they hurried back to the lodge, they were unaware that their every move had been watched. The surveillance cameras had been positioned so that all who entered the perimeter of the grounds would not avoid detection.

The prescribed hour had long passed as they entered the walled garden, calling again to Flora. This time, they were faced with two large mastiffs, their sinister silent presence resembling that of a fox stalking its prey. The stealthy animals had been trained to emit no sound as they paced back and forth, their slavering jaws forming a canine grimace.

Giselle and Inez stood transfixed in terror. As the animals bared their teeth and moved slowly towards them, Inez stepped in front of her daughter like a lioness protecting its cub. Still the dogs remained silent.

Inez, her face drained of colour and her whole body trembling with fear, indicated to Giselle to back away just a few inches at a time, whilst she held the gaze of the more ferocious of the two dogs.

Just then, Flora came out of the potting shed and screamed for Max. 'Max! Max, the dogs are out!'

Just seconds later, a loud whistling sound emitted from nowhere, then Max appeared from around the side of the greenhouses, looking red-faced and shaken.

The dogs immediately withdrew and he threw large pieces of raw meat to them, which they devoured noisily, their jaws slavering and covered in blood.

Inez's fear rapidly evaporated into a spontaneous boiling cauldron of incandescent rage.

She marched at pace past Max into the great hall, commanding Giselle to wait for her in the morning room, and burst into Henry's study without the courtesy of first knocking. He looked up, startled at her lack of manners. Giving her a cursory glare, he swung around on his chair, turning his back to her as he abruptly ended his telephone call.

Inez, her composure in shreds, launched herself into an unprecedented tirade of vitriol. The severe shock of having narrowly missed being mauled to death by her own husband's guard dogs had left her feeling tense and tearful.

'Why do you feel the need to protect yourself with such terrifying brutes?' she demanded. 'What do you keep here to warrant such invasive security?' Her anger mounted. 'Giselle and I were inches away from death! Is that what you want, Henry, then you will be free of any obligation to me?'

She sat down, feeling breathless and deflated. Henry came round the desk and embraced her.

'My dear, do calm yourself. Our location here is isolated, as you are well aware. I deal in almost priceless artefacts, so effective security is of crucial importance to us all,' he said.

She struggled out of his arms. 'Do you realise, or even care, that your daughter might have been maimed or worse today? I absolutely insist that the dogs are kept away from the garden for the duration of our visit.'

Henry looked uncomfortable and tapped his nails on the desk in impatience.

'My apologies, Inez, but I cannot comply with your request. There is too much at stake. I will arrange for a whistle to be left in your rooms. This will afford you the only protection required, as my dogs are trained to contain and hold intruders until we can take control of them.'

He came back to her side and took her hand, 'Now, Inez, to a more pleasant subject. It would please me if you and Giselle would stay here for an extended period. As you know, I must leave early in the morning for Vienna and will not return until the weekend. I want to hear news of Gaston's misfortunes. Perhaps I can be of some practical help in his recovery? When will he be able to join us?' he asked silkily.

His mesmeric gaze felt like a sigh in her heart. She was drowning in nebulous unspoken feelings of tainted love and lust. Fleeting thoughts of her most recent younger lovers assailed her. They had served as a diversion from life's disappointment, leaving a shallow pool of sexual indifference in their wake.

This latest encounter with her husband had stirred her passions. He constantly invaded her thoughts, frayed her nerves, and punctuated her feverish dreams with images of carnal fulfilment. Her fervent desire was that of a renewed bond between them, built on honour, respect, and deeply held affection.

This was her last opportunity to discard the painful memories of their early married life, to rediscover a new understanding between them, borne out of unconditional love.

Henry had chosen her as his wife. In the intervening years of their separation, he had not attempted to alter the terms of their marriage. Conversely, she was unaware that he had always nurtured the hope that their differences would recede over time and that a reconciliation would fill his abyss of loss. But then, there was his captor, Margot.

Inez acknowledged to herself the depth of her passions, but now she must find the strength to execute her as-yet-unmade plan to banish Margot forever.

Inez joined Giselle in the morning room and rang the bell for tea to be served. Max appeared after a few minutes, looking acutely uncomfortable, and apologised again for the earlier unfortunate incident with the dogs. He had the diffident air of a man caught in a web of divided loyalties. He remained resolutely dignified, but Inez found his seemingly furtive mannerisms so annoying that she could hardly contain her temper.

'Max, please ask Margot to serve our tea, as I would like to speak to her.'

She and Giselle sat hardly daring to speak to each other for fear of being overheard.

After some twenty minutes, Margot appeared with a tray on which were arranged cups, a steaming teapot, and individual cakes of an indeterminate flavour.

'Margot, we were walking in the garden this afternoon and found ourselves in the churchyard.' Inez saw the other woman flinch. 'We searched for Simone's grave in order to pay our respects and leave flowers.' Margot's eyes were downcast, her fingers twitching the hem of her sleeve, and an expression of thinly-veiled contempt stole across her refined features.

Inez continued, 'Why was Simone buried in that dark, sad little corner and not in the family vault?'

Margot moved into profile and lifted her head in an effort to conceal her disdain. 'Madame, you should enquire of her father. It was he who chose her resting place.'

Inez shared a knowing look with Giselle and persisted in her questioning. 'Margot, my husband has invited us to stay here indefinitely, or alternatively until my concerns for Honoré's wellbeing have been satisfied and my wishes fulfilled.

Should you require more staff to accommodate us, please feel free to hire them.' Inez walked over to face her rival. 'Please accept that your moon is waning.'

Margot glared at Inez, her face contorted with anger and suffused with colour.

Inez had now crossed an indefinable boundary. Margot unleashed a torrent of suppressed hatred for her, lashing out with such venom, rising like a serpent preparing to strike.

'You! You!' she screamed, 'You will not be allowed to destroy the life I have fought so hard to keep for my daughter. You who have everything, money, connections. You with your childish petulance. When you deserted this house, the blame was laid forever at my door. Only death will separate me from Henry.'

She moved closer, and Inez could feel the pagan supernatural power of her presence. 'You will fail,' she spat, then turned volte-face and left the room.

The two women were transfixed to the spot. Neither of them spoke as they tried to assimilate the scene they had just witnessed.

'Mother,' said Giselle, did I hear correctly when she said *her* daughter and not yours?'

'Just a slip of the tongue, my dear,' Inez lied. She was not yet ready to share her doubts with Giselle, as her pain would be unbearable without Gaston to share it. 'Her illness leads her to believe Honoré is her own child.' She smiled and stroked her daughter's cheek.

Margot is my enemy. Mine to vanquish, and vanquish her I will, she thought.

Inez cautioned Giselle to be discreet and not recount the argument to anyone but Gaston. She would formulate a plan then speak with Henry at the weekend.

Just then, there was a commotion in the hall. A large object, covered in a blanket, was being carried by strangers towards the staircase, in the direction of the north wing.

Max was orchestrating this difficult manoeuvre as the entrance door opened out into a sharp curve. Curiosity overcame the women, so they joined in the procession. The object appeared to be a narrow, long case clock.

Finally, after much manoeuvring, the men eased the object successfully around the long curve of the staircase, along dark labyrinthine passages, and into a bedroom situated at the far end of the north wing.

The room exuded a faded grandeur of an era long past. The wide windows allowed the occupant of the room a stunning, ever-changing panorama of foaming turbulent sea and sky.

Inez, with eyebrows raised, looked enquiringly at Max. 'Well, are we allowed to preview the object?' she asked.

He reluctantly removed the cover. There stood a delicately exquisite, long case clock. The clock face was decorated in mother of pearl, intricate pearl flowers trailing elegantly down its pale lime wood case. It had the unnerving look of a floating spectre.

Inez felt a presence behind her; a whisper of breath on the nape of her neck. She turned sharply to see Margot standing close behind her.

'Madam, I gather this clock is a present for you,' said the housekeeper. 'You will find it useful, as this guest suite,' she indicated with her hands, 'will be yours for the duration of your stay here.'

Inez nodded obliquely. Privately, she was appalled at the mere thought of spending her nights in this wing of the lodge. It was thought to be haunted by a man in uniform, and a shiver of apprehension fingered her spine as she contemplated her fate.

She glanced at the door, hoping to see a lock and key, but there was none. Sliding her hand over the handle, it felt clammy and left a film of moisture on her palm.

She entered the adjacent bathroom to wash her hands, and noticed the elderly ceramic bath was stained, the wall and floor tiles cracked and greasy.

She grimaced. *If this was part of Margot's plan to frighten her, she had certainly underestimated her victim*, thought Inez.

The ill-fitting casement window moved back and forth on the latch, airing the room with salty, pine-scented air. She opened the window and looked out onto the greenish grey, silver-tipped waves of the North Sea crashing through the embrasures onto a walled jetty below.

They formed part of the old fortifications of the building in a time when their enemies had come from the sea to find cannons waiting to repel them.

The bedroom was furnished in the French style – a large armoire with a faded mirror stood opposite the window, reflecting the filtered light. An extremely ornate chest of drawers stood in the other corner, with matching walnut nightstands either side of the bed, and a sofa had been placed in the draught from the window. Inez thought of her luxurious bedroom at home in Honfleur, and offered up a silent prayer in praise of her thermal underwear.

A pale cream and green rug she recognised as Aubusson, complemented the cream silk coverlet and drapes on the half tester double bed.

Two pictures lined the walls – one a portrait of Honoré, painted prior to her accident; the other a copy of a late Picasso, painted after his cubism period, depicting a dark-haired, semi-nude woman languishing on a chaise.

Inez looked thoughtfully at her daughter's portrait. She desperately wanted to believe the young woman she'd met earlier was her daughter, but her intuition told her she was not. And if not, where was Honoré now?

If her suspicions were found to be correct, what other deceptions would she uncover? Henry must know, or had he also been duped by Margot and Simone?

As she opened the door to leave, she thought she saw a dark shadow step back into a recess in the hallway. Inez paused, took a deep breath, and walked on.

Just then, Iona appeared with a vase of Michaelmas daisies in a crystal vase. 'For you, Madam, for your room,' she explained. The scent sickened Inez and she knew who had sent them. How she detested the blooms, and the person responsible for ordering them.

'Thank you, Iona, however you are mistaken,' Inez said with a smile. 'They are my least favourite flower. Take them away, and please ensure that none are placed in the house for the duration of my visit.'

The poor girl looked crestfallen. 'But Mrs du Val said they are your favourite, 'she protested.

'Don't worry,' Inez told her. 'I will speak to her, but remember, no more daisies.'

Giselle appeared engrossed in her tablet. She was conducting one of her endless Facetime sessions with Gaston, her face alight with elation.

'He will definitely be joining us at the weekend. Oh, I have missed him so much. Come and see my room.' She hurried away, leaving her mother to follow in her wake.

They made their way back through the great hall, up the staircase, and on into the hallway of the south wing. Inez was incredulous at the distance placed between her and Giselle. Perhaps this was Margot's method of separating them, or Henry's intention to keep a secret tryst.

Giselle and Gaston had been given a bright airy suite of two rooms – one for sitting, the other for sleeping – and two bathrooms. The smell of fresh winter white paint was evident. A four-poster bed, draped invitingly in pale yellow to match the sofa and chairs in their sun-warmed sitting room, completed the welcoming atmosphere that was so in contrast to the suite allocated to Inez.

Giselle was delighted with her accommodation, but her thoughts were concentrated on her injured husband and their imminent reunion.

Inez, resigned to her bleak tower, was concerned by the absence of a lock on her bedroom door and thought it prudent to keep some kind of weapon about her person.

They left Giselle's rooms and made their way to Honoré's suite, tapping the door quietly lest she was asleep. They entered to find her sitting as usual in the bay window.

Margot once again was seated opposite, holding Honoré's hands. They were deep in conversation and looked up in irritation as Inez and Giselle entered the room.

'I hope we are not intruding,' said Giselle, noting the warmth in Honoré's eyes as she engaged with Margot.

Margot ignored them for a few moments, her conspiratorial expression dissolving at once into one of exasperation at being interrupted. She stood up, kissed Honoré, then sailed past the two women in an air of studied indifference.

Giselle rushed forward. 'Darling, let us take you out into the garden. It is still warm, and I have good news. Gaston is now well enough to join us, and will be here at the weekend. Our family will be whole once more.'

Honoré stared fixedly through the window, her face clouded in despair at the mere thought seeing Gaston again. 'Giselle, I am happy for you,' she said, 'but please leave me. I find your company tiring.'

Giselle drew back, stung to the core by her sister's intolerance.

Inez by now was wilting. She pleaded a headache and escaped to her room to rest before dinner. Henry had been absent all afternoon, apparently on estate business. She settled her weary body onto the sofa in her room with a book and a blanket. Before long, she fell into a deep, dreamless sleep.

When she woke hours later, the room was in complete darkness. Reaching out for her phone, she turned and to her horror saw a shadowy figure. Inez cried out as the figure approached, but it covered her mouth to stifle her scream with its hand, and whispered, 'You are not welcome here. Remain at your peril.' The voice was muffled and unrecognisable.

Her attacker had grazed her face with a ring, and Inez tasted blood on her lips. Shaken and terrified, she attempted to escape her room, but her legs were frozen in fear and would barely move.

She eventually reached the ground floor, then began frantically searching the empty rooms for her attacker or anyone to alleviate her fears. Pausing to catch her breath, she decided to head for the comparative safety of the kitchens.

Her lip by now was throbbing and required an antiseptic salve. She ventured cautiously along the stone passageway, under the old room call bells that were used to summon the servants in the last century.

Iona was preparing dinner, but looked up and smiled. 'Madam, can I help you?' she asked pleasantly.

'Yes please,' replied Inez. 'Do you have a first aid kit? I have grazed my lip.'

Relieved to see a friendly face, Inez sat at the large oak table in the centre of the room and looked around in admiration. The kitchen and laundry rooms had been transformed into a sleek, sophisticated work space, which seemed incongruous in such an ancient building. She began to relax in the enveloping warmth of domesticity; just being around food always made her feel happier.

' Iona, do you live here on the estate?' she enquired.

'Oh no, madam, I have a cottage in the village. When my travelling days were over, I came back home to care for my parents. That was just after Miss Honoré's accident, when the older members of staff were asked to leave.' She gave Inez a knowing look of disapproval. 'They employed new people, none of them locals, and it didn't go down too well in the village, madam,' she volunteered with apparent innocence. 'There was a lot of talk about the goings-on here, but we value our jobs, so we ignored it,' she added.

Inez asked if she kept any medicinal brandy in the kitchen. 'Oh yes, madam,' said Iona, and she reached into a cupboard for a bottle of golden panacea and a glass.

After a fortifying snifter, Inez steeled herself and went back to her room. Fright had dulled her senses, but with alcohol warming her nerves, she felt more relaxed. The air in her room held a faint but unmistakable trace of a perfume she recognised; it was not her own. For the moment, she would keep her fears safe from her volatile daughter.

Inez, now partially recovered from her fright, went into the dismal bathroom to freshen herself, then went in search of Giselle. As she passed Henry's study, she heard raised voices. Evidently Giselle was remonstrating with her father on some matter, and their argument sounded rather heated.

Giselle suddenly came bursting through the door, halting in surprise to see her mother eavesdropping.

'Mother, where have you been hiding? I became completely lost earlier when trying to find your room. Father is being difficult as usual,' she grumbled.

Inez smiled quizzically and the two sought refuge in the morning room. Inez sank into a sofa. 'I need a drink,' she sighed. She had no intention of disclosing the incident in her bedroom earlier that afternoon.

Giselle looked in the sideboard and found a bottle of rather elderly sherry and poured two large glasses.

'Do you think Gaston will make sense of all of this unnecessary security?' she asked. 'What can they be hiding?'

Inez raised an eyebrow but said nothing. After what seemed to be an interminable length of time, they heard a bell informing them that dinner was about to be served.

Max served oyster soup, followed by stuffed sea bream, seasonal vegetables, then lemon soufflé for desert. Copious amounts of chilled Sauternes were consumed throughout the meal. The conversation around the table consisted of polite general enquiries about their health and the progression of their careers.

Margot was conspicuous by her absence, which in turn unnerved Honoré. She looked fretful throughout the meal and ate less than a mouse.

Henry's frequent speculative glances in Inez's direction disconcerted her. *Was he concealing a hidden agenda?* she wondered. Thankfully, Giselle babbled throughout like the proverbial brook, announcing to all in detail the complexities her mother had experienced in running her School of Art.

As the evening wore on and the cheese course had been consumed, both Giselle and Inez were feeling quite inebriated. The potent sherry on empty tummies had taken effect, not to mention the wine, and now they were expected to drink, of all things, port.

When every vacuous conversational subject had been exhausted, Inez decided to retreat to the sanity of their hotel for the night.

She placed her hand on Henry's arm and gazed into his cool eyes. 'We must bid you goodnight. Thank you for your hospitality. We will return tomorrow afternoon,' she said.

Max had thoughtfully ordered a taxi as he considered neither ladies were in a fit state to drive.

At eleven-thirty that same evening, they were both still sitting in the hotel bar with Gaston on Facetime, discussing the events of the day over large brandies. They needed Gaston's strength and vitality of mind to support and navigate them through the difficulties to come.

Max drove Henry to Newcastle Airport the following morning; he was booked on the eight-fifteen flight to Vienna. Persistent drizzle from leaden skies did nothing to dampen his spirits. He was free! Free for the next three days to live his own life away from Margot's prying domination.

His trusted business associates had arranged the usual diversions of extravagant hotels and paid female escorts; Henry relished the prospect of the pleasures and sexual excitement to come.

Settling back in his seat with a strong coffee and an in-flight breakfast he began musing. The only current dilemma in life was the reappearance of Inez.

Her father had tried in vain to prevent the marriage of his only child to a former Nazi activist and sympathiser. But Inez had refused to take his advice, such was her obsession with her prospective husband.

In the past, Henry had needed her father's discreet payments in return for keeping his distance from her. Her inheritance was worth his endurance, if not for himself but for Honoré.

Why did she have to come back, disturbing the past and jeopardising his plans for the future? he thought. *It was obvious she still had feelings for him.* He resolved to manipulate her and not resort to murder unless absolutely necessary, as he was reluctant to ask Margot to poison her. Fortunately, she used untraceable toxins grown in the kitchen garden, which meant her previous victims had been diagnosed as having died of a heart attack.

Margot's unreasonable demands were becoming increasingly difficult to control, though. She knew too much already, and the time was fast approaching when she would need to be dealt with before she turned her murderous attentions to him.

He sat languidly musing on his thoughts, turning over in his mind the similarities in their characters. He and Margot were both ruthlessly selfish, their virile intimate life fuelled by the hypnotic potions made again from the delights of the garden. But he was tiring of her; he was tiring of them all.

Max was his loyal henchman, the lynchpin holding the whole enterprise together. He held the keys to the dark secrets of Roxberg Gate, and was the only person in Henry's life that was non-negotiable.

Inez awoke with a feeling of dread and a monumental hangover. She rose and peered out of the window. Swirling mists and set fret hung over the roofs of the village, like an affirmation of doom.

Conflicting feelings of trepidation and excitement gripped her, regarding their forthcoming return to the lodge. *Should I have left the past undisturbed?* she thought, as she wondered what mischief awaited her in the days to come.

If she asked Gaston to buy a firearm, it would alert him to their danger. He was not fully recovered from the cellar incident, not to mention Collette's poisonous attempt on his life. But of course, he and Giselle were unaware of the ordeal she had suffered in her room yesterday.

She thought it strange that recent tragic events had taken place in so short a time. Was it possible that they were connected in some way? 'Impossible,' she said out loud.

She rang Giselle to say that packing was her immediate priority, and they agreed to meet for breakfast at nine o clock. Just then, her phone rang. It was Max offering to collect them both at two pm.

'Thank you, Max, you are very thoughtful. See you later.' Inez wondered where his loyalties lay. With Margot perhaps? Could he be trusted, or was he Henry's spy?

Giselle was also suffering a hangover; the very thought of food nauseated her.

She was trying to think about the laundry arrangements at the lodge, as there certainly was not enough staff to carry out her personal requirements. She had help at home in Menton.

How very vexing. She decided to befriend Iona, whose no-nonsense attitude to life appealed to Giselle. Furthermore, she had noticed the look on the girl's face when receiving instructions from Margot; there was no love lost between them, Giselle was sure of that.

Over a breakfast of strong black coffee, they both vowed never to touch the demon drink ever again or to avoid mixing grape and grain. 'It was the medieval sherry that caused it,' Giselle groaned, and held her head. She hadn't Facetimed Gaston yet this morning, as he would have absolutely no sympathy for her.

Promptly at two pm, Max arrived to collect them. He struggled to fit their mountainous pile of luggage in the boot, so Giselle placed her vanity case on the seat beside her with her coat thrown over to use as a makeshift pillow.

Inez felt relieved that Henry was absent, as she felt and looked ghastly. *Now we will become the unprotected victims of Margot's torturous behaviour*, she thought.

Her assumptions proved all too correct.

Later, as she walked along the labyrinth of hallways that led to her room, she could smell a now familiar odious scent enveloping her.

Max glanced in her direction. 'I must apologise, madam, they will be removed at once.' As she entered her bedroom, revulsion almost overcame her at the sight and scent of the hated blooms. She rushed to the casement, opened it wide, and hurled the daisies – complete with their crystal vase – out of the window. A shower of yellow pollen covered her hands.

The sound, as it crashed onto the rocks into the foaming waves below, resembled that of a shotgun being fired. She turned to see Margot standing in the doorway, her face white with fury.

Inez strode across the room. 'Margot, why do you persist in this obnoxious behaviour? I can and will have you removed, if it continues.'

Margot sneered, 'You have no power to remove anyone, you have been deceived. You know nothing of our lives here. Be careful, you have been warned.' With a swish of her skirts, she was gone.

Inez turned to Max. 'What did she mean? What is going on here?'

'Madam, I beg you, be very careful. There is evil in this place. You should leave now today. Anything could happen and I would not wish any harm to come to you or your daughter.' He held both hands up. 'Please do not ask me to explain, my loyalties prevent further explanation.' He made a slight bow and withdrew.

Inez sank onto the sofa, her mind in turmoil, a tingle of fear creeping up her spine.

Where was Giselle? she thought, as she reached for her phone. When her daughter appeared, Inez recounted the daisy incident and Max's warnings.

'Well, Mother, I did expect a battle. However, we must stay until we have solved the mysteries here.'

Inez was loath to admit that she felt frightened and violated, but Giselle noticed her reticence. 'If we leave now, Mother, it would be cowardly, and we will always have regrets.' Inez gave her daughter a look of wry resignation then visited the bathroom to wash the yellow pollen from her hands.

They looked out to see the rain had stopped.

'Fresh air will cure our mood. Come on,' coaxed Giselle, 'this time we will take a whistle and explore the beach.'

They remembered to ask Max to secure the dogs, as they dreaded a repetition of their last encounter, and each put a whistle in the pocket of their raincoats in case of emergency.

The path to the tiny spit of grey sand was rocky and very slippery, but worth their effort. The rugged seashore, with its salty scent and white-tipped waves, exhilarated them. Giselle took some images on her phone and sent them to Gaston to whet his appetite.

Inez turned to her daughter. 'This beautiful place has mystical vibrations, perfect for early morning yoga.'

But Giselle laughed. 'You will need thermals, a fur blanket, and a stiffened resolve to exercise out of doors in this climate at this time of year.'

Standing there on that lonely beach, her only thoughts were of her injured

Husband. They had been parted for too long, and she was counting the days to their reunion.

The powerful waves foamed around their boots. The tide was turning and the sun's weak rays had dissipated; they must return or risk being trapped on the rocks.

As they climbed past the walled jetty with its embrasures open to the tempestuous waters, Giselle noticed new iron rings had been inserted into the wall.

She thought it odd that anyone would enter the grounds from the seaward side. The tides were changeable and the treacherous currents required expert navigation. Glancing upward, she saw that the jetty was almost directly under her mother's bedroom window.

'You can indulge your pirate fantasies from your bedroom window, Mother,' Giselle called out cheekily.

They shivered in the late autumn chill and were glad to be heading indoors.

Inez went directly to her room to take a warm bath before dinner. She tried the handles of every door along the corridor which led to her room, but they were all locked.

Giselle wandered down to the kitchens, hoping to avoid Margot. She needed time to ingratiate herself with Iona, who was busy with a mandolin and a bowl of peeled potatoes.

'Hello, are we having dauphinois potatoes this evening?' she enquired.

Iona smiled. 'Yes. Do you like lots of garlic and parsley?'

'Sounds delicious,' said Giselle. Holding the kettle in the air, she asked, 'Tea?'

Iona accepted her offer and indicated where the cups were stored.

Giselle asked if she could help prepping any other ingredients.

'You want my job, do you?' said Iona with a smile.

'Not likely,' replied Giselle. 'I am an atrocious cook. Gaston and I eat out every evening unless he cooks.' She looked rather sheepish. 'Iona, I would love to hear more of your life. I hear that you are a well-travelled lady.'

Iona was taken aback by Giselle's request, as she hardly knew her. She glanced into the hall to check if anyone was listening.

'I live in the village with my fiancé, the village policeman,' she said, her head lowered in concentration.

Giselle caught her breath, understanding Iona's reticence.

'I have the afternoon free tomorrow,' the girl said quietly. 'Come to lunch, if you like. I live at Ebb Tide, the cottage next to the hotel.'

Giselle was elated with this breakthrough. She needed help to learn her family's secrets. 'Thank you, I will look forward to it, and I would love to meet your fiancé if he is free. You understand, this must be our secret.'

That night, after conferring with her partner, Iona decided take Giselle into her confidence by disclosing everything she knew about her employers. She thought it was her only chance of exposing the flagrant disregard the family held for the law.

The staff had all witnessed boats with packing cases being unloaded onto the beach beyond the north wing; locked doors within the lodge, where no-one was allowed to clean, with the exception of Margot; large, dark-coloured vehicles driven by strangers making short visits after nightfall.

Iona had diarised and photographed where possible these suspicious events for the past year, then reported each of them to her fiancé. The timing of these mysterious deliveries was difficult to predict, due to their irregularity, which made the use of camera drones ineffective.

Giselle felt that some progress had been made. Now she must tackle the thorny issue of Honoré's parentage.

The late afternoon dusk was falling as she walked through the unlit rooms and up the stairs to The Vienna suite. After listening at the door for some moments and hearing no sound, she quietly opened the door and found the room empty. Entering nervously, she quickly took the hairbrush from the dressing table and removed all of the hairs, putting them into her pocket.

As she turned to leave, Margot appeared in the doorway. 'Were you snooping or stealing from your sister? It is obvious that she is not here, so why did you linger?' she snarled.

'Margot, I do not need to justify my actions to you,' Giselle replied. 'Move aside, please.'

Margot let her pass, her eyes travelling over Giselle to ascertain if she had taken anything.

Giselle went back to her room feeling pleased with her detective work, if not a little smug at outwitting the odious housekeeper. She ran a bath and fitted her headphones on her head and turned the volume up.

As she lay in the warm bubbles formulating her next move, her phone rang. It was Gaston. Mindful that she might be overheard, she kept the conversation light and arranged to collect him from the airport on Saturday, just two days away. She could hardly wait to receive his ardent attentions.

She fell asleep in the bath, only to be woken by her mother.

'Darling, come along, we will be late for dinner, I am famished,' Inez said as she wrapped a warm towel around her daughter and kissed her tenderly. In less than ten minutes they were walking into the dining room.

The table was laid to perfection, a centrepiece of ferns, twigs and autumn crocus complemented the place settings. Max had placed two bottles of unopened Chablis in a silver ice bucket.

'Gosh, Mother, they think we are alcoholics,' said Giselle. She thought it prudent not to mention her earlier conversation with Iona for the time being. Discretion was vital to her plan, and she was convinced that their conversations indoors were being recorded. She would reveal all to Gaston, preferably in the privacy of a restaurant when they met at the airport.

Margot's icy-faced figure appeared in the doorway. Holding herself aloof, she said, 'I will not now or ever be joining you both for dinner. I cannot speak for Honoré. She will decide for herself.'

Giselle called out to the disappearing housekeeper, 'A wise decision!'

As Margot turned, she almost fell into Iona, who was pushing a heated trolley laden with their delicious dinner courses.

Max appeared to pour their wine. 'Will two bottles be adequate, madam? he said to Giselle with a twinkle in his eye.

She started to giggle. 'Thank you, Max, for looking after us,' she said, neatly avoiding any embarrassing comments relating to her drinking habits.

She found the servant-mistress relationship distasteful and irrelevant to the modern age; she thought it archaic and outdated.

'Tomorrow we will search the house for furniture to create a suitable cosy dining arrangement to be set up in the morning room,' she suggested. 'This room is too ostentatious for daily use.'

They ate and drank until 11pm, their laughter filling the oppressively ornate rooms with the unfamiliar sounds of mirth and conviviality.

Taking the dishes to the kitchen, Inez loaded the dishwasher while Giselle raided the various pantries for brandy and lavender shortbread, made by Iona's fair hands. At midnight, they wearily climbed the stairs, kissed goodnight and headed in opposite directions to their bedrooms.

Inez knew that she had imbibed more alcohol than usual and hoped that it would not disturb her night's sleep. She lay in bed and immediately drifted off to sleep.

In the early hours, she awoke with a start. The room was in darkness and she was perspiring profusely. The loose casement was rattling in a raging gale, its grasping strength gaining purchase on the faulty latch.

She could hear the maelstrom that was the North Sea lashing the rocks below her window. Through a veil of nausea, she saw a movement as the room spun around.

'Who's there? she cried out in terror.

The dark, hooded figure standing in the corner of the room remained still, silent and unmoved, as Inez staggered to the adjacent bathroom, just in time to deposit the food she had eaten earlier into the lavatory.

As she groped for support, her head swimming, she missed her footing and fell, hitting her head on the bathtub. Oblivion descended as she was rendered unconscious.

Margot entered the room behind her with eyes narrowed, a sly satisfied smile on her beautiful face. Silently, she withdrew.

Next morning, when Inez failed to appear at the breakfast table, Giselle went in search of her. She was shocked and appalled to discover her mother semi-conscious on the bathroom floor, with a deep cut to her forehead. It was evident that she had lost a considerable amount of blood, as Inez had used the towels to staunch the flow from her wound.

Brushing aside her mother's absolute refusal to visit the local hospital, Giselle gently bathed and dressed her, then rang for Max to help her into the car. The duty doctor at the hospital advised Inez that he intended admitting her for observation due her head wound, as he feared she might be suffering from concussion. In any event, she could hardly stand. Her face was devoid of colour and her feelings of nausea persisted.

Giselle departed at lunchtime on the pretence of collecting her mother's personal items from the lodge, but drove straight to Iona's pretty little cottage where her fiancé was waiting to greet her.

He seemed affable enough. Shaking her hand warmly, he apologised that Iona had just popped out to the shop and would join them shortly. He invited her to make herself comfortable, then offered her a glass of home-made juice topped up with spring water, as she would be driving home. Giselle would have much preferred wine and water.

In her handbag, she had secreted three envelopes, each containing hair samples from Inez, herself, and Honoré. When she tearfully recounted the tragic events of the past few weeks, his grave expression gave nothing away. He simply listened without comment to her concerns, made notes, and commiserated with her difficulties.

They heard a key in the door, and Iona appeared wearing a sympathetic expression and full of questions regarding news of Inez.

Lunch was served in their cosy, rustic kitchen. Concern for her mother had temporarily deprived

Giselle of her appetite, until Iona produced from the oven a slow-cooked casserole of venison in red wine, roasted butternut squash, and home-grown spinach, followed later by pear and cardamom tart with yoghurt.

Giselle was in heaven at such delicious wholesome food. *Little wonder her father had employed the girl,* she thought.

Iona served coffee in the sitting room, and they settled into deep sofas to talk further of serious matters and to air their grievances.

'Firstly,' said Giselle, 'I have brought samples of my hair and that of my sister and mother for analysis.' She looked tentatively at the policeman. 'My mother and I have instinctive doubts regarding Honoré's true parentage.' She paused. 'May I go on?' He nodded his assent.

'Five years ago, she was flown to a hospital in Switzerland, after suffering a life-threatening skiing accident in Austria. She remained there for ten months, apparently having undergone three operations to reconstruct most of her body,' Giselle explained.

'Whilst we appreciate the trauma of the accident and bearing witness to her sister's death has irrevocably altered her appearance and persona, neither Mother or myself can find any remnant of the girl we both knew and loved.'

The police officer nodded thoughtfully. 'You may be required to formalise this conjecture, as we do not conduct tests without good cause,' he told her.

Giselle understood, and agreed to accept his help and good advice.

'The authorities have had the lodge under surveillance for some time,' he confided. 'So far, we have been unable to gather enough evidence to further our investigations. Your grandfather was a lifetime member of a far-right organisation, and we suspect your father of continuing the business of fencing stolen artefacts after his death.

'We believe – but, mind you, we have no proof – that your father is a vital link in a worldwide chain of art thieves and is using the lodge to store valuable items before they are sold on to the highest bidder.' It was his turn to pause. 'Giselle, my dear, you are in a position to help us. Are you prepared to assist us by gathering evidence against your own father?'

Giselle was stunned. She felt her whole world was falling apart. She would be condemning her father to years in prison if their suspicions were founded. She looked down to hide her tears, but nodded. 'I have gone too far now. We must discover the truth.'

She rose wearily and thanked them both for their hospitality. 'I must attend to Mother's needs,' she explained.

Giselle rang Gaston before driving back to the lodge, giving him her devastating news. He cautioned her to take great care. 'Cook your own meals and wear gloves indoors, as there are many ways of distributing belladonna,' he warned.

In some trepidation, she began her journey. If her investigations into her father's business affairs became known, she would be placing all of their lives in danger.

Giselle calmed herself and tried to behave normally. When she arrived at the lodge, she was greeted by Max, who was most solicitous in his enquiries after her mother's health.

'I have returned to gather her personal items, as they are keeping her in for observation tonight,' she told him.

'Very good, madam. Will you be dining at home tonight?' he asked.

'Max, for the present, my arrangements are uncertain. Basically, I will look after myself for the remainder of my visit. Thank you.'

She collected her mother's nightwear and toiletries, then set off back to the hospital. Stopping halfway down the drive, she looked at the lodge reflected in her rear-view mirror. Tears welled then began to flow.

Her home had the façade of a fairytale castle, similar to those found in Bavaria. Today, glistening in the autumn light, its majestic forbidding turrets represented not only a threat to those she held dear, but to the person she imagined herself to be.

On her arrival at the hospital, a doctor called her into his consulting room and invited her to take a seat. He looked rather serious, and Giselle held her breath.

'I must inform you that your mother has been poisoned with belladonna, or deadly nightshade as it is sometimes termed,' he said gravely. 'She will stay here until we have ascertained how she received the substance, and in the event of foul play, a criminal investigation will be launched.'

Giselle felt her throat constrict; she felt sickened. They had come here to heal wounds and build bridges, but instead had found iniquity on every level. She immediately resolved to take her mother out of harm's way and return her to the safety of her home at Honfleur. She would never be allowed to return. When her mother recovered, she would discuss the sensitive subject of divorce.

Giselle stayed with her mother until late into the evening. Inez slept through most of her visit, giving Giselle time to gather her courage and make plans.

Back in the lodge kitchen with Iona late that evening, she scrambled eggs for them both. The two women sat and talked in whispers of their lives, loves, and what the future might hold for them both. They hoped their conversation had not been overheard.

They agreed that whatever the outcome of the difficult times ahead, they would face them together and always remain close friends.

Giselle washed the supper plates then made her way up the scullery steps leading to a vestibule at the side of the lodge. She heard the courtyard clock chiming the hour. *Ten o'clock; much too early to retire to bed,* she thought. In any event, she felt wide awake.

Finding the oppressive silence and permanent chill of the house depressing, she wandered along a corridor to the main reception rooms. *How could anyone exist in such a gloomy place? So different from the South of France,* she thought.

Perhaps this would be a good opportunity to conduct a little detective work of her own. She checked every ground floor room for signs of life. She considered the arrangement of furniture and pictures impersonal, similar to that of a museum.

She looked around for family photographs, but disappointingly, none were displayed. She cautiously ventured into her father's study, leaving the door slightly open as she had only the refracted light from a small lamp in the hallway.

She crept over to his desk, then quietly and with great care, tried each drawer. To her great disappointment, they were all locked, except one.

It contained a variety of false passports, all with her father's images and unrecognisable names. Legions of keys were piled on top of each other with address fobs clearly marked. She extracted her phone from the pocket of her jeans then photographed the entire contents of the drawer, then heard a noise in the hall. Someone was coming. Standing quickly, she composed herself.

Margot dissolved into the shadows. She was wearing a close-fitting black dress, making her difficult to discern in the dim light, but her signature perfume lingered on the air, confirming Giselle's fears. If Margot had witnessed her activities, she was in grave danger.

Giselle sent the images of her evidence via email to Iona's fiancé. This alone would be enough to convict her father of wrongdoing. With mixed feelings, she made her way back to the sanctuary of her room.

Drawing the curtains, she opened the casement and leaned out. The sharp sea air stung her face, but she was glad of it. *I have just condemned my own father*, she thought, tears of anguish streaming down her face. 'Oh Gaston, where are you?' she called out, her words lost on the rising wind. Feeling lost and disconsolate, she mused, *here are no doves of peace, only predators of love.*

That night, the moon was full. Its magnetic allure suffused her with a surreal hypnotic desire to float away from her inner feeling of betrayal. She slept fitfully, occasionally crying out in her limpid slumbers.

The early morning light from a pale silver dawn woke Giselle, the urgent cries of gulls urging her to rise and start the day.

The room was icy cold, and she ached from her cramped night's sleep on the sofa. She had been too frightened to undress and go to bed. She made her way to the bathroom, hoping a hot, reviving shower would lift her mood.

This was the day she had been longing for. She would collect Gaston from the airport this afternoon, allowing her ample time to visit her mother beforehand. She kissed her wedding ring. Today she would dress to excite her husband.

Giselle eagerly immersed herself in preparation for Gaston's arrival, in total ignorance of the storm that was about to break over her head.

Margot had indeed witnessed her prying in Henry's desk. A tiny camera had transmitted Giselle's image to the estate office beyond the kitchens.

When Henry rang that morning to confirm his flight arrival time, Margot informed him of his daughter's devious activities. 'Do you want me to deal with her?' she asked.

'Certainly not!' expostulated Henry. 'Keep away from her. I will deal with her myself.'

Margot had grown accustomed to the high ground in their relationship. Her detailed knowledge of Henry's unlawful activities had imprisoned him in her power.

She retreated to her suite for the rest of the day, her unstable mind in its usual state of silent turmoil. As she paced back and forth, a sense of impending doom assailed her.

She had a pathological fear of the dark reaper, the shadow of his scythe hanging over her. She prayed at midnight to a horned creature to save her and her daughter.

Henry was an easily dispensable narcissist. His disobedience would not be tolerated, and if he resisted, he would no longer exist.

Margot's loveless childhood had been fraught with difficulty. Her parents had been declared unfit to raise two little girls so young and close in age.

The sisters were taken from their French homeland to live with a great aunt in the isolation of the Scottish borders. They grew and thrived under the watchful but uninspiring eye of their religiously devout maiden aunt.

When they were sixteen and seventeen respectively, the younger of the pair returned to her native France in order to help her parents cultivate their newly-planted vines and olive groves. Margot had stayed to seek a position as a trainee chef in the country that she had grown to love.

One day, Henry Roxberg called in to visit her aunt, to collect items of rare fine china that were no longer of use to her. He strolled into the kitchen and happened upon Margot preparing dinner. Her beauty took his breath away, and he lusted after her body in the same way as he devoured her delicious food.

On her eighteenth birthday, he offered her the position as his housekeeper. She accepted the position on a temporary basis, as she had plans to continue her studies. It was her fervent hope that one day she would open a restaurant of her own.

Henry's seduction of her had been swift, stormy, and possessive. He beguiled her with his talk of marriage, children, and their future together.

Setting her own ambitions aside, she acquiesced. As the years passed, she began to lose confidence in her own abilities, and consequently her sheltered world shrank under his auspices.

She lived for Henry. His thoughts, wishes, and whims subjugated her existence.

On occasions, when having taken aphrodisiacs, she would broach the subject of his unkept promises, but he took his pleasures then brushed her concerns aside.

Her tenuous threads of love weakened, only to be replaced with silent revenge. She concealed her ambitions, played his game, and kept him sweet, but eventually she knew she would win.

Embittered resentment likened to seeds of hate grew within her heart, allowing the unstable side of her nature to resurface. As the years passed, when none of Henry's promises had materialised, she decided to have his child in the vain hope that he would honour her.

When at last she became pregnant with Simone, his attitude towards her changed significantly. He would offer vacuous excuses regarding his lack of funds and then disappear to the continent for weeks without informing her of his whereabouts.

Margot was three months pregnant he arrived back from a business trip to Madrid and broke the news that he had met the daughter of a wealthy industrialist. The girl's mother had died recently and left her fortune to her only daughter.

Henry found her Latin looks attractive, but nothing more; he preferred slim Nordic blondes.

He disregarded Margot in assuming that she would forgive his duplicity. He professed that she was his only love and that he would protect her and their child forever. Thereafter, she hated him with a vengeance, and vowed he would pay – in blood, if necessary.

Giselle caught a glimpse of him through the crowds of people walking towards her. She ran forward to the barrier to keep him in her line of sight.

He appeared more svelte, his strides shortened by a slight limp. She melted into the depths of the intense feelings flooding her body with desire, tempered by protective love for him.

Then he saw her waiting expectantly, her face a radiant beacon of excitement. They embraced, clinging to each other, drawing solace from their fevered kisses and drowning in the familiar scent of their bodies. They were both oblivious to the sidelong glances they were attracting from passers-by.

Giselle had arranged a room for the night at the hotel in the village, to enable them to discuss their news in private and make love in secure surroundings.

Numerous lengthy Facetime conversations had been shared between them during the past two weeks, but there was one piece of information that Gaston had withheld from her.

He kept a soft reassuring hand on Giselle's knee as she drove to the hotel. He was unable to take his eyes from her, and made a silent promise that they would never again be separated.

They checked in and made their way upstairs to the bridal suite. Giselle found this rather amusing, as they had been blissfully married for the past ten years. Gaston had no such thoughts, and found it rather appropriate under the circumstances. He just couldn't wait to fulfil his obligations.

He held her at arm's length and looked deep into her eyes. She could see that he was close to tears.

'We must never again be parted, not even for a day. Your absence has been torture to me,' he murmured.

'Yes,' she sighed. 'Life is unimaginable without you, my love.'

The hotel was quiet and peaceful, as the cool late autumn days had sent seasonal tourists scurrying back to their day-to-day lives. Giselle sat looking out of their window. The woodland garden had captured the burnished glow of fallen leaves, and she imagined them as a pool of dying embers. As an artist, she appreciated beauty in all its forms, but nature was her first love.

Gaston had no need of a bridal suite to consummate their reunion. An under-stair cupboard would have sufficed, such was the intensity of his ardour.

His lack of stamina was not reflected in his performance. Nevertheless, his incomplete recovery proved a hindrance, as he tired easily. He lapsed into a ubiquitous post coital nap as Giselle stroked and kissed his head affectionately.

As he slept, she lay quietly on the window seat so as not to disturb him. Presently, she too surrendered to her dreams, but after half an hour she woke feeling refreshed.

Tiptoeing past her sleeping husband, she ran a jasmine and lime oil-scented bath, then placed a bottle of chilled champagne, two glasses, and a dish of marshmallows on a small table beside the bath.

Gaston had been planning, not sleeping, and he entered the bathroom at the moment of her disrobing. She stepped like a Venus into the scented water, pausing to allow him time to absorb the sight of her opulent beauty.

Their mutual seduction was usually conducted in an unselfconscious silence, however there were occasional exceptions.

Reclining, legs slightly apart, she began provocatively caressing her sex. Catching his breath as his body convulsed in lust, he disrobed to reveal his throbbing arousal glistening with moisture at its tip.

Gaston leaned over to lick and finger her navel, casually moving to her ripened nipples. She leaned to tease his excitement with her tongue whilst stroking the tender valley between his legs with a soft red feather.

Their bodies secreted a subliminal aroma of pheromones, permeating their senses with an intense, insatiable hunger to indulge in their unusual pleasures.

Through a fragrant mist of steamy tantric ritual, he enticed ripples of ecstasy and release from the depths of her loins.

Their lovemaking continued until late into the evening, neither wanting to leave the marital bed, and eventually they slept entwined until dawn.

Giselle opened her eyes. Immediately, her mind returned to the fascinating disclosures of the previous day and the part she had played in them,

Gaston stirred beside her. She smiled contentedly, drawing reassurance from the warmth of his body. She was no longer alone. Together they would overcome life's obstacles and face their destiny.

She rose and brewed tea for them both. Hearing her mobile phone ringing, she dived under the bed to search for it. It was Inez, asking her to book a room – well, preferably a suite – at the hotel for an indefinite period. She said she had no intention of returning to Honfleur until justice had been served and mysteries solved. She had scores to settle, and refused to leave until she had achieved her goals.

Feeling famished, Giselle chose a biscuit from the tray. After taking a reviving shower, she lay on the sofa near the window, waiting for her husband to rouse himself.

She had considerable difficulty in assimilating Gaston's shocking news that the gendarmerie in Menton had informed him Collette and Margot were indeed sisters. It seemed they had been conspiring together for years with the intention of defrauding the family by exchanging information back and forth across the Channel, waiting for an opportune moment to advance their as yet unknown plans.

Collette had been detained in custody, awaiting trial. She had been refused bail so could no longer pose a threat to anyone.

Margot, of course, was still ever-present amongst them, and had proved she was capable of anything.

Over breakfast, they skimmed the newspapers and watched the soft rain punctuating the swirling sea mist. Giselle ate smoked salmon with scrambled eggs and toast, while Gaston took the rare opportunity of enjoying a full English breakfast.

She watched him devour his food with relish. He had understandably lost weight since Collette's attempt on his life.

Authentically-grown, organic produce played a large part in both their lives, as they both lived to eat. Their confirmed belief in good nutrition and strenuous exercise, coupled with a dislike of conspicuous ostentation, formed the cornerstone of their daily lives.

Giselle's thoughts turned to her father. She was still oblivious to the fact that Margot had watched her taking images in her father's study.

She was dreading their seemingly unavoidable return to the lodge and being subjected to Margot's incessant vitriol. Although, admittedly, she was curious as to how Gaston would react to these violent outbursts.

After vacating their room, Giselle went in search of the owner of the hotel to thank her for her assiduous attentions. She had arranged to collect Inez from the hospital, then drive her to the safety of the hotel, where a quiet and secluded room had been prepared for her.

Life had progressed so quickly for Gaston in the years since his last visit to the lodge. He had completely forgotten just how bleak and foreboding the building appeared to a casual visitor.

It stood in isolation, shrouded like a sleeping dragon, the air dampened and chilled by a heavy sea fret. Rooks cawed from the turrets, creating a sinister, unearthly atmosphere, as if time had stood still within its confines and the rules of a civilised society did not apply here in this place of wanton greed and murder.

No, Gaston thought, *they had all gone too far this time. They must be punished. His revenge would be sweet, and the dish would be served piping hot. Retribution would be theirs to savour.*

Max reached the airport just on time to collect Henry. He noticed two police officers standing to the side of the arrivals hall, their eyes scanning the inbound passengers as they stood in the queue to have their passports checked by customs officers.

He saw them move forward as Henry approached the desk. His fears mounted as he watched while they arrested his lifelong employer and friend.

Giselle had betrayed her father to Iona's partner. Margot was right. They now posed an imminent threat that could not, would not, be tolerated.

Henry was astounded to see the police officers approach him. They politely invited him to accompany them to a small office, where they cautioned then arrested him on suspicion of receiving stolen artworks.

The profound shock and full force of their accusations sent Henry into a spiral of panic. With a clenched jaw and fists outstretched, he lunged at the police officers, his futile anger rising to boiling point. In his confusion, he dropped his briefcase.

'How dare you detain me!' he shouted at them.

When their struggle was over, he was handcuffed and escorted from the building and into a waiting car. Henry was duly informed that a search warrant had been granted for his home and business premises.

Max knew he must escape and leave the country without delay. He withdrew to a safe distance, waiting for the police car to disappear, then drove at speed back to the lodge, leaving his employer to face the music alone.

He almost collided with Gaston and Giselle, who were driving through the main entrance gates. On reaching the fortress door, he turned to survey them both, a look of undisguised anguish on his crumpled features.

Then, directing a severe penetrating look directly at Giselle, he said, 'I have just come from the airport, expecting to collect your father and deliver him to the safety and comfort of his own home.' He continued to stare at Giselle, his eyes piercing into her.

Gaston had stood listening to this exchange with increasing irritation. 'Max, just get to the point, please,' he prompted.

Max drew himself up to his inconsiderable height, turning on her. 'Your father has been arrested by two police officers.' His voice now laden with venom, he continued, 'They were waiting for him in the airport. This is your doing, you stupid bitch. Your persistent interference in our business has destroyed decades of careful planning. I am giving you notice and will be leaving within the hour.'

Gaston smiled and shook his head. 'No, Max, you will be staying here, as I am sure the police will want to interview you.'

Max, in his anger, charged at him, but fell heavily on the stone floor. As Gaston had deftly sidestepped the attack, they all heard an alarming crack of a bone breaking, and Max writhed on the floor in agony.

'Well, Max, the door in your avenue of escape has just closed,' said Gaston wryly.

Giselle rang the emergency services, requesting both police and ambulance assistance.

Gaston turned to his wife. 'My love, your family and their accomplices are all rogues,' he said.

She smiled. 'Not quite all, my love. We still have much to discover. But I fear we have only just scratched the surface. Stay with Max. There is something I must discuss with my sister.'

Crossing the great hall, she ran upstairs.

They were trapped, she thought, *in a macabre web interwoven with so many lives.* For her own sanity and her mother's freedom from her odious husband, she must discover the truth.

Giselle ran through the labyrinth of dimly-lit passages leading to the Vienna Suite.

Exploding into the room, she was confronted by a touching tableau of Margot protectively enfolding the girl, believed to be Honoré, sitting in her wheelchair with a shawl over her lap.

Giselle circled the room, never taking her eyes from Margot's face. This was her long-awaited opportunity to scorn and ridicule the woman who had caused her mother so much anguish over the years.

Surveying the scene before her, she could hardly contain the breath heaving in her chest. Turning to address the younger of the two women, she said, 'I have submitted hair samples from us all for analysis. This will establish what I have suspected since my arrival here, that you are not my full blood sister.' She moved closer, blocking Margot's exit. 'I believe that you are Simone. There is nothing in or about you that I recognise as Honoré. We will exhume that poor forgotten creature lying in the churchyard, and prove that you are an audacious imposter.' She towered over the girl. 'Tell me what happened on that mountain. Did you push her, or lead her off-piste?' Giselle was screaming now, unable to control her anger.

The girl lowered her head and began to weep. She rocked back and forth in her misery, burying her face in the shawl. Meanwhile, Margot stood sentinel behind her, an expression of suppressed rage contorting her perfect features. The girl continued to sob loudly, looking occasionally up at Margot, not daring to speak.

Margot advanced slowly towards Giselle. 'You will have to answer to your father for your wickedness,' she snarled. 'He will never forgive your betrayal of him.' She was sneering as she imagined her power to be absolute.

'Margot,' said Giselle, a little more calmly, 'my father has been arrested at the airport and is now in police custody. And very shortly, Max will be joining him. It will soon be your turn to be questioned and be held accountable for your actions.

We are aware of your relationship to Collette, and your conspiracy to infiltrate our family for your own financial gain.'

Margot's face paled as she fell back into a chair, her eyes rolling in their sockets as she tried to come to terms with Giselle's appalling revelations. Her whole world was collapsing in ruins around her.

They heard a commotion downstairs; the police and ambulance had both arrived. Max had apparently broken a hip and elbow in the fall. The paramedics gave him an injection for his pain, but still he screamed in agony as they carried him away on a stretcher.

Everyone was asked to assemble in the dining room, while a team consisting of four men and women conducted an initial search of the locked rooms in the north wing.

The police officers confiscated the contents of Henry's study, including the false passports and keys from the desk drawer, and informed Margot that she was not to leave the house or indeed the country.

Iona had heard most of the conversations from the warmth and comfort of the kitchen table. She felt her settled world was disintegrating around her.

When all was quiet, she ventured out of the comparative peace of the kitchen into the reception rooms. The air felt clammy, like the lull before a storm.

The rooms were empty, as Gaston and Giselle had disappeared to their room to unpack their belongings. Returning to the safety of the kitchen, she took solace in preparing dinner for them. She decided to employ the time-honoured remedy of chocolate cake to salve the wounds and lift the mood of the largely depleted members of the household.

As she began mixing, the centrifugal motion of spoon against bowl soothed her mind. Soon the aroma of chocolate permeated through the ground floor rooms.

Gaston was first into the kitchen, offering appreciative compliments and cutting two generous slices of the warm, oozing confection. He brewed a pot of fresh mint tea and delicately prepared a tray of matching crockery, then asked Giselle to stay with Iona.

'It's a cliché, I know, but there is safety in numbers,' he explained.

He carefully carried the tray upstairs to the Vienna suite where, as usual, Margot was on guard, and unceremoniously ordered her to leave. 'Please, Margot, go. And stay away until I give you permission to return.' She darted a knowing look at the girl and withdrew.

Gaston placed the tray on the table then settled into the chair opposite.

He smiled and held the girl's gaze. 'Please don't be afraid,' he said. 'Help me to understand your life.' He proffered the cake and tea. 'Do you like the china? I brought them from France, especially for you. It would please me to see you use them.'

They exchanged pleasantries, and gradually she began to visibly relax. When they had finished their tea, he cleared the table then took her hands in his and leaned closer to her. Her latent passion for him rose, illuminating her features.

'I must advise you that for your own sake you must tell us the truth about the accident,' he said, and his expression of gentle concern began to melt her resistance. 'If it pains you to speak of it in person, I would urge you to write a statement or dictate the whole episode into your tablet. Here is my mobile phone number. If you feel threatened or frightened, please ring me, as Giselle and I will not be leaving until this unholy mess is resolved to our satisfaction.'

She nodded, weeping silently, her head lowered. He gathered the tea tray and left her to her grief. As expected, Margot was sitting on a chair in the hall, waiting for him to leave.

He turned to her. 'I pity you and your wasted life. You are a poisonous woman, and you deserve and will receive no mercy.'

Iona was deep in conversation with Flora and Giselle when Gaston returned to the kitchen. The young girl's face was full of concern at the police presence in the house. The events of the day had also disturbed the dogs. They had been enclosed since last night and were becoming increasingly restless in their unaccustomed confinement. Flora had fed them, but they needed their freedom to exercise at will.

Gaston asked her to accompany him to the animals' enclosure; being a dog lover himself, he envisaged a run along the beach would calm them and expend their energies.

Flora, overcome by anxiety, had failed to mention the procedure of blowing a whistle to maintain control over them.

When Gaston reached the animals' compound and saw the two dogs, his bonhomie failed him. Any stranger in their domain would have been faced with a similar response. Their menacing purpose was to warn intruders and protect the occupants of the house, together with its valuable contents.

Gaston decided he would ask the appropriate authorities to remove them, with a view to finding the magnificent animals a good home. He felt sure they had served their purpose admirably, but he was unwilling to risk having them near the family or their dwindling members of staff.

Giselle came in search of him. 'Come along, darling. I have something of interest to show you.'

They took the path out through the kitchen garden, which led on down into the churchyard. The light was fading, the birds settling into their lofty roosts for the night. The stale air stank of decaying vegetation, slippery damp moss coated their shoes, and an atmosphere death hung over them like a black velvet cloak.

Giselle wrapped her coat closely against the early evening chill as she led him to the sad little epithet that was purported to be the resting place of her dear sister, Simone. Gaston genuflected then made the sign of the cross. He considered himself a good Catholic and was unselfconscious in his display of it.

Giselle's mobile phone had been ringing constantly that day. First, it was her mother inviting them to dine with her at the hotel that evening, as she was desperate to hear the events of the day.

Then the police officer in charge of their case had called to inform her that a team of specialist art experts would be with them the following day. They planned to stay at the hotel in the village until they had concluded their investigation.

Their futures as individuals would change irrevocably when the secret stores of art treasures were discovered behind the locked doors in the north wing.

Iona was the unwilling gatekeeper of their secrets. She carried the intolerable burden of knowledge concerning her employers' crimes around with her, like the overflowing pockets in an old dress. Now, as these crimes were about to be revealed, she would be released from any residual personal guilt.

Her only concern was that the police might perceive her former reticence to come forward as collusion, making her an accessory to their crimes.

She decided to remain silent and watchful. The police would gain entry to the locked rooms eventually.

The incriminating evidence that Giselle had discovered had been removed from the desk in Henry's study. Simple logic would point the finger of suspicion in Margot's direction.

Gaston, finding himself alone and curious, wandered off to explore the north wing of the lodge in greater detail. He found the doors in the refurbished areas locked; presumably the police had taken the keys. He felt reassured the rooms would be thoroughly investigated when the art experts arrived in the coming days.

The cavernous rooms in the older parts were accustomed to the relentless assault of howling winds and gales from the sea. They had been abandoned and left undisturbed in layers of dust and decay for many years. A steely grey sky could be seen through the cobweb-framed, ill-fitting windows in the ancient serpentine corridors.

Giselle scurried back and forth down the empty corridors seeking her husband's whereabouts, her silhouette creating moving shadows as she walked along using the compass app on her phone to navigate her direction and calling out to him. 'Oh finally, there you are. Wait for me, please,' she said breathlessly.

He kissed her. 'Come along then, but please take care,' he said.

They came upon a narrow passage which led up to a flight of time-worn steps, leading to a sturdy oak door.

Gaston tried the well-oiled handle. It turned easily in his hand, revealing yet another shorter flight of steps.

They led into a turret which overlooked the sea, then on to another seemingly never-ending gallery, with window seats along the seaward side.

Giselle looked out to see crested waves crashing incessantly against the rocks below, spraying white foam over the stone walls of the lodge.

They came upon a well maintained, iron-studded door. Evidently someone had cleaned the area, as the steps were free of dust and debris. A small wooden box lay on a window sill; inside the box was a key.

Gaston inserted it into the lock, exchanging speculative glances with his wife. 'Here goes,' he said.

Once again, the well-oiled lock turned easily, and the door swung open with a groan on its iron hinges. They stepped into a large vaulted chamber that lay directly under the conical turreted roof of the north wing.

Golden prisms of refractive light flooded through three large stained-glass windows.

A heavily-carved four poster bed stood on a dais, its draperies of pale green watered silk were identical to those in Inez's private sitting room at Honfleur.

A large silk rug almost completely covered the wooden floorboards and was of a similar colour; even the coverlet was identical to the one Inez slept under each night.

Giselle went over to touch them. Perplexed, she turned to Gaston. 'It's unreal.'

They stood in amazement. 'How could he have copied Mother's furnishings? How could he know, and why would he?' Giselle asked.

'Perhaps one of her students had been his spy,' suggested Gaston.

Baffled by their discovery, they began to examine the room more closely. They turned their attention to a large mirrored armoire standing in the corner of the room. Giselle went over and unlocked it.

She gasped when she saw the contents. Hanging encased in cotton dust covers were six neatly-pressed uniforms belonging to the Third Reich, their medals polished and glinting in the light.

Boxes containing press cuttings and photographs of people she did not recognise lay alongside shining black boots at the base of the armoire. Giselle was devastated.

'So, the rumours were true.' She looked at Gaston, anguish written clearly on her face. 'My father is a monster, and in my eyes beyond redemption.'

Her mouth was set firm and stubborn as she continued. 'This is too shameful for me to bear. Please let us leave this to the authorities.'

So absorbed were they in their unspeakable discovery, they had failed to notice a dark shadow silently enter the room behind them.

Margot stood watching. She carried a small silver gun, a silencer fitted to its barrel. The maniacal sneer on her face left them in no doubt as to her intentions. She raised her hand and aimed the gun at Giselle.

'You should have stayed away,' she said, 'and heeded my warnings. It is dangerous to pry into our affairs. This is where it ends for you all,' she said menacingly.

The next few seconds appeared to happen in slow motion. To their amazement, Iona appeared behind Margot with an iron skillet in her hand and brought it down on Margot's head. As the woman fell forward, her face contorted in pain, a shot rang out. Fortunately the bullet just missed Giselle's head and travelled into the armoire.

Gaston rushed forward, white with fright. In anger, he snatched the gun from her hands as she lay on the floor, blood pouring from her head. He tied her hands together behind her back with his belt, then began staunching her head wound with his scarf.

'Well, madame,' he said, 'you have shown us your true colours, as if we hadn't guessed. Do me the courtesy of staying alive, as I will be glad to see you waste away in prison.'

Anger ripped like arrows through his body. At that moment he thought himself capable of anything in order to protect his wife.

Giselle called out to him, 'Please stop, she is unworthy. Leave the poor insane creature to the police.' She had already collected herself and dialled 999.

Iona looked stricken. 'Have I killed her? Oh no, is she going to die?' she cried. 'I only intended to stop her, not kill her.'

Margot regained semi-consciousness then proceeded to moan and curse in her struggle to free her hands. Her verbal tirade at being confined continued unabated, thus confirming their belief that she was completely deranged.

They locked her in the turret, nursing her sore head, but Gaston became so impatient for the police to arrive that he rang them again, stressing the urgency of his call.

Giselle went in search of Honoré, or whoever she purported to be. She found the young woman in bed, looking drained and tearful.

Giselle sat on the bed and took her hand. Looking directly into her eyes, she patiently explained that her mother had been involved in an accident so would be unable to assist in her care for the foreseeable future. Giselle said she would arrange for Flora to be her carer and companion until more a more permanent solution could be found.

Strangely, the girl seemed unconcerned at the prospect of her mother's absence. 'It may not be necessary,' she said. 'I will speak with Margot before deciding. When can I see her?'

'My dear, it may be some time, as the police are involved.' Giselle hesitated. 'Your mother tried to kill me. If Iona had not come to our rescue, Margot may have killed Gaston, too.'

Honoré looked at her in disbelief and shook her head. 'I always feared something like this would happen. This is the end. I have had enough of deception and heartbreak. Later, we must talk. I have much to explain.' She looked imploringly in Giselle's eyes.

Flora, when informed of her new temporary duties, was crestfallen at leaving her garden to the mercies of a stranger, only to find herself cooped up indoors with her introverted friend and no means of escape.

They all heard the crunch of car tyres on the gravel drive then an urgent ring of the doorbell. Gaston rushed downstairs to admit what appeared to be legions of police officers, two with firearms strapped to their belts. He led them to the door of the turret where he had imprisoned Margot, then left them to deal with her.

The detective in charge of the team requested a few minutes alone with the family. He was a tall, slim fellow. In conversation he avoided prolonged direct eye contact with anyone, his eyes darting around as he spoke. He assumed the manner of a Victorian patriarch.

They sought privacy in the morning room, but he politely declined coffee and biscuits. 'This, madam, is not a social occasion,' he said. 'However, thank you for your hospitality.' His look was serious and uncompromising.

He explained that the various investigations might take weeks and enquired as to their future plans. Not waiting for a reply, he advised Giselle to remain in England in order give evidence and to assist in their enquiries.

He claimed the added burden of Margot's iniquity would take time to assimilate, and that they should prepare themselves for a lengthy stay.

Gaston entered the room looking exhausted. He entrusted a set of keys to the detective, enabling him to proceed with his enquiries unhindered by their absences.

Giselle recounted her earlier conversation with the detective, including his instructions for them to remain indefinitely at the lodge. This unwelcome news left Gaston feeling depressive and trapped.

Suddenly there was a sharp tap on the door. Without waiting for a response, an officer entered, looking grave. The man swallowed firmly in an effort to control himself, as everyone's attention fixed upon him.

He faltered as he gave his account of finding Margot – a woman he had admired since childhood – lying on the silken bed, her face a mask of death.

On her breast, a locket lay open, an empty file in her hand. She had taken the poison she had so often administered to others. The officer had conducted a simple mirror test and felt her pulse, all to no avail.

The detective made another phone call, this time to the forensics team for assistance. He looked to the ceiling for inspiration. 'These events are unbelievable,' he said. 'I have known this family for many years.' With that, he left the room.

The shock of Margot's suicide had left them all feeling crushed and somehow ashamed. 'Did someone once say "how the mighty fall"?' offered Flora, in a brief flash of juvenile wisdom.

Giselle was experiencing great difficulty in coming to terms with the tragedies of the last few weeks. Her delicate nervous system was unused to such tragic events.

She had become increasingly fractious and overwrought as their eagerly anticipated visit had rapidly descended into a nightmare. She had come to heal rifts and build bridges. Instead she had been subjected to every evil sin that life could hurl at her.

In a mood of extreme agitation, she rang Inez, asking her to call a taxi and join them immediately as she had important diverting news to impart.

When Inez arrived, looking expectant and ashen-faced, Giselle took her hand then gently told her of Margot's suicide. Inez began trembling.

'We have killed her,' she said. 'If we had not come here, she would still be alive. What am I to say to Honoré?'

Inez felt no triumph on hearing the downfall of the woman she had found it impossible not to hate. Margot had been party to every deal and transaction that had passed through Henry's business. Now Inez knew for certain that she had blackmailed him into continuing their relationship.

Characteristically, her first thought was for Henry's welfare. She feared he might suffer a breakdown if his punishment was severe. *Would he be able to withstand years behind bars after the life he had been enjoying until recent events had overtaken him?* she wondered.

The responsibility of Henry's current state of mind had been passed wholesale onto Gaston's shoulders. Giselle had given him the onerous task of breaking the news of Margot's death, as she and her mother were unwilling to face him.

Inez immediately asked to view the corpse. The two women had been sworn enemies, but it was unthinkable that one of them would be driven to such an act of desperation and finality, brought about by their devotion to Henry.

Giselle studied her mother for signs of added stress. She decided to keep a watchful eye over her, as she feared Inez might suffer a further setback to her recovery.

The leaden atmosphere was slightly relieved when Iona entered the room and reminded them all that they had missed lunch. Giselle looked at her phone; it was 2pm.

'I have laid a buffet in the dining room for everyone, and filled the drinks tray,' said Iona. She thought they all looked in need of a stiff drink after the shocking event that had taken place earlier that morning.

Giselle and her mother napped by the morning room fire for the remainder of the afternoon, awaiting the dispersal of their lunchtime alcohol intake to dissipate. Later, they travelled back to the hotel to pack and collect Inez's luggage. She again bade goodbye to the hotel manager, managing to escape before any gossipy enquiries could be made.

Inez decided on a more convivial suite, as she had felt isolated and lonely in the north wing. She had left numerous personal items in the room she had occupied on her previous visit, and went to collect them. She ran quickly, knowing Margot's body still lay in the turret, awaiting removal.

In her bedroom stood the pretty long case clock with the mother of pearl face. She paused to study it closer. The pendulum was still, and no sound could be heard from the movement. An envelope lay beside it, containing very precise instructions as to how the clock should be packed for its journey, together with her address in Honfleur and the winding key. She put the key in her handbag for safe keeping.

Yes, she thought, *I will accept this gift. It will look beautiful in my sitting room.* Before dusk, they took Honoré to pay her last respects to Margot before her body was removed to the mortuary.

Inez looked upon the woman that had caused her so much anguish and felt nothing but pity. She had escaped from the claustrophobic life imposed on her by Henry, whereas Margot had been his captive. She'd spent her whole life in pursuit of the unattainable. Perhaps the tendrils of Margot's love had run deeper than her own, after all.

She would divorce him, Inez thought, *then sell her home at Honfleur.* The ghastly memory of finding the box containing Maude's little body at her front door would never fade.

She would buy a villa in the hills above Nice to be nearer to Giselle and Gaston and reinvent a new beginning for her own sanity. She loved life and intended to live it on her terms.

Now, she thought, *it was time to focus her attention on Honoré.* The poor girl had lost the family on whom she depended, and was in dire need of physical and emotional support.

Inez held a deep compassion for the girl. The shock of losing her mother in such devastating circumstances had sent her into a near catatonic state of mind. The test results from the hair samples had been incontrovertible.

Since their arrival, Honoré had taken every meal in her room, refusing the entreaties of her family to join them. Only Flora could reach her.

Inez dreaded the thought of exhuming the remains of the body lying in Simone's grave. Her every instinct told her it was Honoré, her brave, lost daughter, who lay buried in that desolate place.

There was a tap on her door. Iona popped her head round the door to inform her that the police had now removed Margot's body and that Honoré was asking for her.

Gaston and Giselle had disappeared to the beach to breathe fresh, salty air and clear their heads.

Inez went to the kitchens to make a pot of fresh mint tea. She sliced two portions of lemon drizzle cake for herself and Honoré, in the hope of engaging in a meaningful conversation. The girl was alone and defenceless now. Surely she would cooperate with her own family?

Thoughts were circling Inez's head as she climbed the stairs whilst attempting to balance the heavy tea tray legs on her hip.

On entering, she found the room empty. Putting the tray on a table near the window, she called out, 'Honoré, where are you?'

'In the bathroom. Just a moment,' came the reply.

Inez recoiled in astonishment to see Honoré glide elegantly into the room wearing a slim-fitting black dress and heeled court shoes. The late afternoon sun sent prisms of light through her billowing clouds of dark hair.

At first, Inez could hardly believe her eyes. Then she became very angry. 'Well, I can see now that your infirmity was a charade. Your whole existence is a pretence. You are not my daughter and I intend prove it.'

The girl sat down and calmly poured their tea. Handing Inez a full cup, she smiled. 'You are correct,' she said with callous defiance. 'I am not your daughter. Honoré died in the accident. You may never accept the truth when I tell you that I did not push her. In fact, I almost lost my own life trying to save her. We were as close as full blood sisters. I adored her so much. She was the only person to love me for myself.'

She paused briefly before continuing. 'I am tired of the life my mother forced me to live these past five years. When Honoré died, I was trapped in her insidious web of lies. Her ambition for me to inherit Henry's wealth and villainous legacy made my life a never-ending misery. She thought he owed it to her for marrying you.'

Inez felt nauseous. She stood abruptly and left the room without another word. Walking quickly, she made her way out of the lodge and down into the churchyard, collapsing in tears onto her daughter's grave.

She clung to the headstone, calling out to her long dead daughter, tears rolling down her cheeks, saturating the bodice of her dress. Gaston found her there semi-conscious, her hands bleeding from grasping the stone. She looked up to him with reddened eyes.

'I have been misled and mentally violated in my own home,' she cried. 'They will be forced to regret this day. I will seek retribution for their treachery and burn this devil's lair to the ground.' She was out of her mind with grief. 'They let be believe my daughter had lived. How could Henry allow his daughter to be buried in this disgusting hole?'

Gaston lifted her gently and helped her back into the morning room. She lay on the sofa until morning, refusing to eat or change her clothes. There remained, encased in her misery, for two days.

Giselle, always a firecracker ready to fight a cause or right a wrong, came to her mother's aid.

She visited her father, who had remained in police custody since his arrest. He had been refused bail on the grounds that he was likely to abscond.

Henry's attitude towards her was distant and icy cold. 'You were always a liability,' he told her.

'Father, did you ever consider the consequences of your actions?' she asked.

'No, of course not.'

She shook her head slowly. 'Your arrogance is breathtaking,' she said.

He refused to discuss the situation, past or present, in respect of her mother or Margot, and denied any knowledge of Simone's impersonation of Honoré.

Giselle believed him, though. She now understood that his all-encompassing self-importance excluded anyone of no use to him.

He asked to see Inez, saying he owed her a profound and unreserved apology.

'You will never see my mother again,' replied Giselle. 'She has vowed to destroy every trace of your vile business.'

Henry smiled. 'No, my darling daughter. She will carry a part of me with her forever. Every time she looks at you, she will see me.'

They all ate together that evening. Iona and Flora had been invited to join them, and even Simone appeared. She looked rather shame-faced but relieved to be released from a lifetime of pretence. They felt little compassion for her, but she was in mourning and alone, so Giselle invited her to stay and dine.

Inez, having willed herself to carry on, had given Iona the afternoon off and enjoyed having the kitchen to herself. Cooking had always been a salve for her troubles. She indulged herself in a flurry of culinary activity, and had cooked up a storm in the kitchen all afternoon.

She had made a divine casserole of pheasant with seasonal vegetables from the kitchen garden, followed by apple charlotte and chartreuse cream. Their sorrows were duly submerged in French Chablis and copious amounts of brandy.

Simone said that she had spoken with her cousin Claude and informed him of her mother's death. Her Aunt Collette had been convicted of conspiracy and attempted murder; she had also confessed to poisoning little Maude.

Giselle was tempted to set upon her in retribution for her cruel and heartless deceptions, then changed her mind, castigating herself for her unseemly thoughts.

After dinner, they carried their brandies through into the morning room. The main topics of conversation were the unbelievably tragic events of the past week.

Giselle found it hard to believe that only three weeks before, her tranquil, well ordered life had been about to change forever. *Now, decisions must be made, and soon,* she thought.

Finally satiated and exhausted from endless chatter, they wearily climbed the stairs in the early hours, promising not to reassemble until lunchtime the following day. That night, they all slept the sleep of the dead.

The dawn rose as Gaston stretched and leapt out of bed. The clock read six-thirty. Looking out of the misted windows, he sighed. The weather was abysmal. A raging sea sent swirls of fret up around the turrets. Undaunted, he crept around the bedroom, dressing quietly so as not to wake Giselle.

He went downstairs into the boot room where his oilskins were stored. He was no stranger to early morning beach walks. It was at times such as these that he missed his little Maude. Perhaps at some point he would feel able to face buying another dog.

His sombre mood of yesterday lifted as he walked along the beach. It was just a fraction in size of the shining gold sand of Menton. How he longed to be at home with Giselle, living their own lives away from this animosity. He was unwilling to practise his usual asanas in such an inhospitable climate; handstands and a run would have to suffice. He took deep breaths, filling his lungs with salty air, then began to run.

When he returned, Simone and Iona were sitting in the kitchen, chatting and drinking coffee. Inez was nowhere to be seen, so he went up to her room to enquire as to her health and temper. Tapping on the door, he awaited her response. On entering the room, he found her resting on her pillows, engrossed in her laptop.

He need not have concerned himself. Inez said that she had been awake for most of the night, sending email instructions to her notaries, asking them to place her house at Honfleur on the market.

She had seen three potentially suitable properties advertised for sale, mostly situated above the city of

Nice, and all having stunning views of the Alps Maritime. Appointments had been arranged to view them later that week.

He cheekily perched himself on the end of her bed and asked to hear of any other plans that she had kept from them. She laughed and scolded him for his impertinence.

'Seriously, my dear,' she began, 'there will be big changes here, as I intend to sell this house. It is tainted with mischief and greed, and I want none of it.'

They read the house details together, then Gaston persuaded her to join him for breakfast to enable her to elaborate further.

Giselle awoke to find herself alone. She longed for Gaston to stroke her breasts and soothe her body. Soon he would notice the changes to come. The secret of her unborn child was hers to cherish. She must wait until an opportune moment presented itself to reveal her life-changing news.

She showered then, glancing in the mirror, noticed a new curve around her tummy. 'You're mine,' she whispered, 'just for a little longer.' She smiled and stroked her tummy.

The art fraud police arrived at eight o clock, tablets charged, ready to inspect the artefacts contained in the locked rooms in the north wing.

Henry had accrued an extensive collection of fake paintings awaiting a contrived attribution, genuine antique furniture, crystal and rare china, all of which needed to be catalogued and photographed. The officers set about their task diligently, making use of the kitchen and ground floor conveniences as their own, leaving the family with the impression of being guests in their own home.

Inez became increasingly offended by the officers' snide innuendos regarding the extent of her knowledge or involvement in Henry's business affairs. They made it their business to misinterpret her every comment, however helpful.

I *Dam them* she thought. *How dare they insinuate that I was complicit in this infestation of evil.*

The aftermath of her family's misfortunes, brought on by their own dishonesty, sickened her. She would escape to France, if only for a short time. *A new home complete with a new life*, she thought exuberantly.

They all met for breakfast, including Simone, who looked decidedly perky dressed in jeans and a bright red jersey. Giselle refused to partake until Simone had changed to a more suitable black ensemble.

Inez retorted that the arrangements for Margot's funeral were the sole responsibility of her daughter, and that she would definitely not be attending the service.

Gaston wore the long-suffering look of a fish floundering out of water. Henry had issued vehement instructions that Margot was not to be buried on the estate, and had adamantly refused her internment in the family tomb.

'Well! This is just the first of his orders that I will disobey,' retorted Giselle. 'The church won't have her, she is a suicidal outcast. No, she will be buried in that miserable hole vacated by my sister when her remains are moved to a more fitting place... as far away from Margot as possible,' she said determinedly.

They all turned to Giselle aghast. 'My mind is made up,' she said. 'I will make arrangements today. A requiem will be held in our family church, and Simone will choose the order of service.'

That said, she cleared her plates then headed for the kitchens.

Simone followed her, loitering in the doorway. She asked if criminal charges would be brought against her. Giselle gave her a long hard look before replying.

'No, no charges. Consider yourself fortunate. Eventually you would have been found out. Your play acting was poor and so transparent.'

Giselle went on, 'Where will you go when Mother has sold the estate? You should be making plans. I would suggest you live with your grandparents. They have a holiday cottage in their olive grove. Why not plant a vineyard? We will invest some funds when this place is sold.'

Simone's expression travelled through a wide emotional spectrum as Giselle spoke. She was not averse to returning to France, or receiving the funds to start a business.

'Can I trust you to keep your word, or are you saying this to be rid of me?' she asked.

Giselle rounded on her. 'Trust? How dare you insinuate that my ethics mirror yours! I would suggest a call to your grandparents would be in order, with a view to arranging a very long stay. I will explain your absence to the authorities after your arrival in France. Now, be gone, out of my sight. I find you repellent,' Giselle added, viewing her with distaste.

Simone smiled to herself as she returned to her suite. *I have prevailed*, she thought. *I am free at last*. She lost no time in ringing her grandmother at Ypres, her fascinating disclosures leaving the poor woman in a state of shock.

'I will explain further when I see you,' she added. 'Please ask Claude to ring or email me. I am so looking forward to seeing you.' Ringing off, she could hardly contain her excitement. She would depart immediately after her mother's internment.

Inez was impatient to view the properties she had seen online before other buyers snapped them up. She rang her friend in Rouen, suggesting they meet at Nice Airport. Her friend readily agreed; the pair were like-minded and enjoyed each other's company. She offered to book a hotel in the historic quarter, close to the restaurants and shops.

Inez had an urgent desire to escape from the oppressive atmosphere prevalent in the house. Giselle had mentioned in passing that Henry had asked to see her. Her intuition told her that he wanted to apologise and to talk of the future. Her conscience would not allow her to leave the country without first making her peace with Henry. It was a meeting she dreaded, as she intended to inform him of her decision to divorce.

Giselle entered the room and was amused to find her mother clothed in cashmere wraps and sitting under the covers for extra warmth.

'What are you planning?' she asked, sidling over. 'Come now, don't be coy.'

'My darling,' began Inez, 'this tiresome episode must end. I am homesick. Life here is alien to me. I have decided to divorce your father and move to Nice, but please don't imagine that I will be on your doorstep at every moment.'

Giselle took her mother's hand and kissed her softly on her cheek. 'Mother, I am with child. My dearest wish is to have you close by me.'

Inez clasped her firmly, tears peeping from her eyes. 'Oh, how I have longed for this moment. Does Gaston know?'

'Yes, Mother.'

Just then, he walked in, his face shining with pride.

'We must celebrate,' announced Inez. 'Bring our finest champagne.' She put her hand up, but smiled at Giselle. 'Not you, my darling.' She looked thoughtful. 'Ah, this explains why you left your wine last night,' she said.

Gaston eased himself onto the chaise and rang down to Iona in the kitchen, requesting champagne and four glasses. he asked her to fetch Flora from whatever messy task she was performing in the garden, then to come upstairs to Inez's bedroom.

Inez looked up. 'Oh, should we include Simone?'

'Definitely not,' said Giselle, then recounted their earlier conversation.

Flora appeared wearing her decrepit gardening clothes; Iona had been baking bread, and was coated in flour. Gaston proposed a toast to his beautiful wife and their unborn child.

'Happiness and tragedy are strange bedfellows,' commented Inez. 'We have recently experienced too much of one and not enough of the other. Now I have no excuses. I must visit Henry.'

Gaston asked them all to stay and listen to the proposition he was about to make. All eyes focused on him, his audience was waiting.

'There are certain aspects of this visit that I will miss when we return to France, namely you two lovely, honourable ladies.' Flora blushed, and Iona just looked curious. 'Iona, I would like to offer you the position of manager at Café Villande. I took the liberty of speaking with your partner last night, and he is agreeable to a new life on the continent. You, too, Flora. Perhaps you might find a husband to delight you.' He smiled.

'I will not attempt to pressure you both,' he went on.

'You won't have to,' interjected Iona. 'The answer is yes!'

'Me, too,' said Flora.

They sat in stunned silence, as though a wave had washed over them, cleansing away their anxieties.

'What a lovely idea,' said Inez. 'Gaston, you really are a genius.'

He drank his champagne and looked, quite frankly, smug. Not only had he managed to recruit trustworthy staff, but he had found solutions to all of their most pressing problems and had himself become a father-in-waiting.

The prospect of these exciting developments injected a sense of gaiety into their every crevice. Conversations around the table became humorous and playful, each of them anticipating with pleasure their new lives together.

The fateful day arrived. Inez's reluctance to visit Henry had taken her to the edge of an emotional precipice, but no-one could ever accuse her of moral cowardice.

She had considered leaving the matter with a solicitor in England, but to her relief, Giselle offered to accompany her and offer support.

The two women were not allowed a private conversation. With a guard standing within earshot, the news was more difficult to impart and Henry's hearing of it more wounding.

His defensive reaction was typical of him. His usual offhand manner was replaced with self-righteous self-pity. 'You have abandoned me when I need you most,' he bleated.

She, in turn, was incredulous, considering the outrageous transgressions he had visited on her for the entirety of their marriage.

He was an unfeeling monster and must accept his punishment with well-mannered grace, thought Giselle. She wondered if he would suffer the same fate as Margot. How could a man of his sensibilities cope with prison life? Might he also consider his life to be worthless?

Giselle's faith in the opposite sex had undergone some dramatic changes as her relationship with Gaston evolved. His intuitive approach in calming her headstrong nature with a combination of kindness, genuine affection, and sexual fulfilment, instilled in her feelings of completeness. She placed her hands on her unborn child and vowed it would never know the dark secrets of Roxberg Gate.

On their return journey, they called into the vicarage to keep a pre-arranged appointment to organise Margot's funeral, together the exhumation of Honoré's remains and her subsequent internment in the family mausoleum.

Giselle, in bristling fashion, was prepared for difficulties to be presented. However, none came, and the vicar was most obliging. *He probably knew far more about the situation than he disclosed,* she thought.

Inez requested that her daughter's internment be delayed for one week, as she had urgent appointments in France.

The house, on their return, was a flurry of activity, cars parked everywhere, people milling to and fro removing items and putting them in vehicles under Gaston's supervision. He had been given a complete inventory and estimated value of the artefacts to be taken. Almost every item contained in the north wing had been stolen or misappropriated in some way. The one exception was the clock with a pearl face which Henry had given Inez as a parting gift.

Prior to her departure for Nice, she had asked for it to be packed as per Henry's written instructions, and shipped to Menton. Gaston gave his assurance that he would keep it safe until she had found a new home. He was relieved to see the stolen artefacts leave the premises, as the family would never recover any credibility until the stains of the past were washed away.

Gaston visited his father-in-law in prison and gave the joyful news of his impending fatherhood. Henry wept bitterly at his own misfortune. The unpalatable realisation that he would be facing many years in prison were unbearable.

'I would rather be shot than suffer the loss of my freedom,' he told Gaston.

He asked if someone would bring him a loaded gun, then his misery would be at an end.

Gaston was furious. He completely lost his temper and was asked to leave. As he turned to go, he shook Henry's hand, saying, ' I will not return. You deserve your fate.' With that, he left, never to see his father-in-law again.

Inez suggested dining in the hotel that night. She was happy to answer questions from the gossipmongers thereabouts. 'I would rather they hear the truth from me now,' she said. 'When Henry's trial begins, the facts may be reported inaccurately.'

The regulars were all in that evening. Perhaps the word had spread after the table had been booked.

Inez left funds behind the bar for everyone to join them in a pre-dinner drink, then she gave a brief explanatory speech and mentioned that the lodge would be sold when the police had concluded their enquiries. Her only regret, she told them, would be leaving her daughter's grave.

'She loved these parts, and would have wanted to remain here,' Inez told them.

The next morning, Inez was up bright and early. She had arranged a taxi to take her to the airport, rather than disturb anyone. Looking out at the undulating countryside, seen through a veil of soft rain and sea mist, made her homesick for France.

How she longed for the balmy climes of the continent. She felt exhilarated as the plane took off, and ordered breakfast, then studied for the umpteenth time the details from the notary. She was not convinced that any of them would suit her requirements. *Not to worry*, she thought. *The hotel in Nice would be an ideal escape for the moment.*

Her thoughts turned to that dreadful day when she had found Maude's dead body on her doorstep. At that moment, she had decided never to return to her seaside home. A blank page in a new chapter was to be her cure.

Returning to Honfleur would be too painful. If others thought she was running away, then so be it. She knew her own mind and it was made up.

Her friend from Rouen was waiting to meet her on arrival. 'I have so much news, good and bad, I hardly know where to begin,' Inez cried.

They had appointments that afternoon with a notary's representative, viewing two properties in the vicinity and three more the following day. Inez, impatient with excitement and glowing with happiness, proclaimed, 'I am to be a grandmother next summer. This calls for a celebration.'

Both ladies were only too familiar with the delights that Nice had to offer. Leaving their suitcases at the hotel reception, they walked the short distance to the market and restaurant area, and within ten minutes were enjoying oysters and champagne. Inez spoke at length about the dangerous difficulties her family had faced at Roxberg Gate. Although she tried to make light of the grisly goings-on, even she could hardly believe her own words.

'Basically, I have bolted,' she told her friend. 'The situation became intolerable. I am expected to return in a few days to attend my daughter's second funeral; the one who died five years ago.'

The immobilière collected them at the appointed time then drove them out of the city towards the hills. En route, he enthused about each villa, assuring her that he would find the right property for her. She accepted his comments at face value as his handsome appearance appealed to her. By 5pm, they had viewed the assigned properties, but none had ignited her enthusiasm.

An arrangement was made to meet the following afternoon to view the other villas on his list. Both women felt in need of a shower and a power nap. They decided to meet in reception at 8pm, then go out on the town in search of fun and food.

Lingering too long in the exotic surroundings of the restaurant, drinking wine and talking incessantly of their plans for the future, kept them out later than anticipated. The scents from the flower market bathed the silky evening twilight in a heady aroma. Inez felt at home, if not at peace.

Walking, arms linked, back to the hotel, they arranged to meet at 2pm in the hotel reception the following day. That would allow them both time to recuperate after their late night and to shop in the Galleries Lafayette.

The representative from the immobilier met them at the hotel at 2pm prompt. He looked and sounded enthusiastic, and was sure Inez would choose one of the properties on offer that day. The two ladies rolled their eyes as they climbed into the car. At the end of the appointment, no suitable property had been found, as they had either needed a complete restoration or the location was unsuitable.

Inez suggested they break for tea at Villefranche-sur-mer. She had never visited the town and was curious to explore its viability as a permanent home.

To her delight, she found it charming. She was drawn to the industrious port, with its busy shops and restaurants of every type. 'I think we may have discovered a gem,' she commented to her friend.

When the waiter brought their tea, he accidentally spilled a drop on the property details. Mopping their paperwork with a cloth, he asked if they were searching for property in the area, and went on to mention that his brother had just completed a sympathetic refurbishment of a traditional merchant's house further along the quay.

Inez looked up in dismay as large spots of rain threatened a deluge. The cosy café tempted them to stay longer for more delicious tea, but they agreed out of courtesy to view the property.

The waiter rang his brother to alert him of Inez's impromptu appointment, and they eagerly set off in search of the house, supposedly just a few minutes' walk away.

Inez immediately fell in love with the large imposing property on sight.

The house faced the lively port. *She could introduce an art school,* she thought, *as the house was too large for one person.*

'Plenty of space for guests,' said her friend.

The garden was smaller than she had hoped for, nevertheless it would suit her needs – there was just enough space for a pavilion.

She rang the owner, asking him to meet her the following day to learn more about the house and agree a price. She would have preferred Gaston and Giselle's opinion before committing herself, but that would be impossible as Margot's internment had now been arranged for the following day.

Inez felt exhausted. The rapidly evolving events of the past few weeks had drained her strength. It was time for relaxation, visits to art galleries, and enjoying whatever life had to offer.

The following day, Inez hired a car, and she and her friend drove back to Villefranche to take a more detailed look at her new home.

She was even more enamoured this time. Fortunately, the kitchen and bathroom fittings had not yet been chosen, enabling her to make her own choice.

Mutual negotiations with the owner proceeded favourably. Eventually they agreed a price, and the owner indicated that it would be at least two weeks before she could finally take possession of the house.

They exchanged details of their notaries. Inez, feeling elated at having found a new home so soon, thanked him warmly, assuring him she would be in touch with her choice of fittings by the end of the week.

As they were talking, she could hear her phone ringing in her handbag, but ignored it and carried on with the conversation. It rang so many times that eventually she walked over to answer it.

'Mother, at last!' said Giselle. 'I have been trying to contact you for hours.'

'What is it, my darling, are you unwell? What has happened?' said Inez, feeling her face flame and heart quicken in anticipation of hearing bad news.

'How can I tell you? This morning, your husband, my father, was found in a pool of blood in his cell. He had secreted a piece of cutlery, and cut his wrists,' Giselle explained. "When Gaston visited him recently, he expressed a wish to end his life rather than face the indignity of a trial and a resulting lengthy prison sentence.

'They may hold an inquest, as he died in police custody,' Giselle continued. 'Should you feel able to attend his funeral, I will endeavour to delay the service.'

The line went quiet. 'Mother, are you there?' Giselle asked.

Inez had dropped the phone and fainted. Her friend picked it up and said she would call her back.

When Inez had recovered sufficiently enough to be driven back to the hotel, she went to her room and stayed there for two days. Never usually one to lament, lament she did, loud and long.

As she reminisced about the past, her father's words came back to her time and again. She was still unaware that he had paid Henry to keep his distance from her.

She had loved her unreliable husband to distraction, but he had simply dashed her love against the rocks lying at the foot of Roxberg Gate.

Her wealth had attracted him, nothing more. In reality, his heart belonged to Margot. She understood him; she was his type.

Inez felt obligated to return to Northumberland. She was unwilling to leave the arrangements to Giselle in her condition. Her two-day sabbatical had restored her strength, and now she felt able to withstand the heartbreak that lay ahead.

She booked her flight. Gaston would collect her from the airport.

At least I can look forward to a new home and a grandchild to cuddle, she thought.

Gaston's vain attempts to lighten her mood were received with a mixed reception. As they drove out of the airport, his thoughts returned to the day of Henry's arrest.

Inez had become increasingly embarrassed by the whole episode. 'My marriage was a sham,' she confided. 'First, I was duped, then cheated. Henry has always made his own arrangements, even in death.'

As they entered the driveway, Giselle came out to greet them. The lodge loomed over her like some great spectre, freezing mist threaded through its turrets like ghostly fingers.

'Darling, this is quite definitely my last visit to this doomed house,' Inez said as they hugged.

'I have a roaring fire and a splendid meal awaiting you,' said Giselle, hugging her mother.

Inez looked at her in mock horror. 'Who cooked it?' she asked.

'Iona,' confessed Giselle ruefully.

Tucked into a corner of the great hall stood a tall packing case.

'I had your clock packed by professionals, as per Henry's instructions,' said Gaston. 'I understand it's your parting gift from Henry. It is due to be collected by the shipping agents later today.'

'Actually, I love the pretty clock,' Inez admitted. 'It will compliment my new home.'

Gaston nodded. 'I will store it in my showroom until you have moved. From tomorrow, Flora will be living in the café. She is going on ahead to house-sit for us until this unpleasant business is concluded.'

With Inez back in residence, decisions could be made, but two funerals and one re-internment would remain their top priority. Iona's casserole of duck tasted absolutely gorgeous. She had made a bitter lemon steamed pudding, and topped it with crème anglaise laced with vodka. After dinner, they settled by the morning room fire to discuss their news over a brandy or two.

Gaston remarked that had he been pre-warned of the havoc wreaked by their visit, he might have stayed at home and avoided the whole tragic episode.

His seemingly insouciant attitude was, in essence, a reflection of his personal armoury. In fact, his tender heart would take many years to come to terms with the events of the past week.

Daybreak was late the following morning, thus everyone slept longer.

That afternoon, they would inter their enemies; retribution and moral justice had been served. Their legacy of painful memories would haunt the family until their days' end.

Gaston's habit of rising early and taking a run before breakfast, had been disrupted of late. Today, he was more in need of the beach than ever.

He mixed then drank a green smoothie. His morning ritual of mindful yoga and healthy eating was completely lost on Giselle. Now, he had the perfect excuse to persuade her to take a more responsible attitude to her health.

In contrast, she preferred to rise later, brunch being the first meal of the day, quite often accompanied by a small glass of wine. It was a practice he now tactfully discouraged.

He went back to their room and placed a small glass of smoothie on her nightstand, kissed her tenderly on the forehead, tucked the bedclothes around her, and made his way down to the deserted kitchen.

The heating oil had run out and it would be days before the next delivery. It would be its last, as far as he was concerned, however long it took to sell the place. It could fall into ruin before he lifted a finger to prevent it.

He shivered as he drank an espresso. The house had the atmosphere of a mortuary. The bodies of Henry and Margot would be returned that day; the church service would be combined and short in duration, under the circumstances.

Henry would be laid near his father and Honoré. Margot was destined for the dank hole that Honoré had previously occupied.

The large pine tree that had shaded Honoré's remains for the past five years, would now play host to Margot's. An area where moss scented the still air with death and decay, relieved only by winter hellebore and snowdrops, was to be her memorial.

With help from the parish priest, Giselle had arranged for their tiny church to be decorated with greenery entwined with lilies, taking care to ensure the stamens were removed for her mother's comfort.

Three cadaverous holes had been prepared, with their straps inserted for the dignified lowering of the coffins. An undertaker from the village, who had had little input into the proceedings so far, had been employed to assist with the strenuous task of moving the coffins.

Gaston climbed into his oilskins then set off for the beach. His thoughts once again turned to little Maude. Perhaps if he bought another dog? Not of course to replace her; no, that would never happen. A companion for the baby? *Yes*, he thought.

Their beach was private, so when he rounded the rocks that separated the two spits, to his surprise he saw a large motor launch moored to the concrete quay which Henry's father had installed many years previously.

Something told Gaston not to intervene. He turned and started running back to the lodge, his panic rising as he had forgotten to check the lock on the quay door.

It's locked, he thought. *I locked it myself, and the key is in the hall.* He ran through the kitchens, passing a startled Iona who was preparing breakfast, through the hall, and up the stairs. His heart was beating in his chest.

Claude had already gained access to the house through the quay door which led up a wide stone staircase leading into the north wing. A large key was hooked to the leather belt tied around his waist.

Inez was sleeping peacefully. She had not heard his stealthy footsteps as he crept into her room. He looked around, as if searching for some specific object, then hovered over her, momentarily savouring her beautiful countenance.

He adjusted his shoulder gun holster and balaclava, then left as silently as he had entered. Moving further down the corridor, he systematically inspected every empty room in turn, unaware that he was being watched.

Gaston, unarmed, was almost too terrified to breathe. His throat constricted and, sweating profusely, he waited until the figure had reached the top step of the staircase, then like a force of nature he threw the intruder headlong down the stairs. The man careered down the staircase onto the stone floor below, while Gaston followed furiously angry and white-faced.

The figure lay unconscious. Gaston removed the gun from its holster and tore off his balaclava. He drew back in shock at the sight of Claude, his former waiter, lying before him, blood oozing from a head wound. Without hesitation, he rang for an ambulance and the police.

In the meantime, he ran to check on Giselle and Inez, who had both slept throughout the whole incident. It occurred to him that in defending his wife and family, he might have committed a criminal act. Incarceration at this point in his life would be as unbearable to him as it had been to Henry.

He sat on the floor waiting for the ambulance to arrive, his eyes fixed on the lifeless body of Claude, a man he had once trusted.

This house is nothing more than a vipers' nest of conspiracy, he thought. *It was incredible that both families had been blithely unaware of the malicious underworld in their midst.*

What was Claude searching for? The house was virtually empty, except for well used furniture of little value.

When the police arrived, they confiscated the gun. They had already alerted the coastguard, who was now en route to collect Claude's boat, still moored against the north wing.

Claude slowly began to regain consciousness, to Gaston's profound relief. It was thought that whilst he was very bruised, he had not suffered any broken limbs, which was lucky for him. However, Gaston would have liked to question him then punch him in the face.

Claude waved his legs like a beetle trapped on its back and screamed in pain.

'Serves you right, Judas!' spat Gaston.

If I stay here much longer, Henry will make a criminal of me, too, he thought, as he mounted the stairs once more to find Giselle.

Iona put the bacon under the grill and kept her thoughts to herself. So impatient was she to start her new life in France, all other considerations had been cast aside.

Gaston was asked to present himself at the station that afternoon, to make a statement. He looked up at the officer and smiled. 'We are burying three members of my wife's family this afternoon, perhaps we could postpone this until tomorrow, if you wouldn't mind.'

The officer offered his condolences. 'If you extend your stay, it might prove necessary to install a permanent office up here,' he replied with a grimace.

Inez and Giselle found it unnecessary to question Gaston about the finer details of the early morning drama, as Iona had given them a full account over coffee and her legendary bacon sandwiches.

Gaston, scenting breakfast, entered the room. 'A little hero worship would be appropriate here,' he said ruefully, 'although a bacon sandwich will suffice for now. Perhaps I should have been a private investigator,' he remarked airily, 'instead of an art dealer.' He smiled as he hugged his wife.

Appetites satiated, they all disappeared to their bathrooms to prepare for the next ordeal of the day. The hotel catering people had arrived and were busy erecting tables in the dining room, where a blazing fire had been lit in readiness for the wake.

The funeral mass had been arranged for 2pm. Numerous mourners assembled in the tiny church, avid for spectacle and gossip, but they fell silent when confronted with the sight of three coffins. The lilting voices of the choir singing Alegri's *Miserere* stirred their emotions to tears.

Many years of suspicion and distrust were cast aside to be replaced with compassion and sympathy for the fast-dwindling family members.

The priest gave a thirty-minute address, referring to each of the deceased in turn. Gaston thought it interminably lengthy, as in any event two of them were not only lapsed Catholics but had throughout their lifetimes regularly broken all of the ten commandments, either singly or collectively.

Giselle gave him several dark looks and squeezed his hands, as you might a naughty child, in order to curb his fidgeting.

She was dreading the moment of Honoré's re-internment, her sister lost forever in this desolate place without relatives to care for her grave. As tears of anguish clouded her eyes, she turned to Inez and whispered, 'My regrets for her will follow me forever. I should have been here for her.'

Inez also found it necessary to contain her demons. Later, in years to come when they were all happy again, she would tell them the absolute truth, the truth she had kept buried in the depths of her heart for so long.

'I need a brandy,' said Gaston, as they entered the dining room. Thankfully, Giselle had ordered a hot buffet to be served.

Mourners spilled out into the hall and sat on the staircase, directing their curious glances everywhere. None of them had previously gained entrance to the gardens let alone the lodge.

As dusk spread its chilly blanket of violet-tinged sea mist along the gardens, the mourners began dispersing. When they had all gone, Gaston invited Iona, her fiancé, and Flora, to join them in the morning room. They lazed in front of the fire, drank heady red wine, finished off the nibbles left over from the wake, and planned their exciting new lives at Café Villande.

Flora would have the bedsit in the basement. Iona and her fiancé would live in the staff flat over the showroom. Iona had decided to let her cottage to tourists, while retaining the option to quell any feelings of homesickness by returning occasionally to visit her family and friends.

Inez's thoughts were elsewhere, her mood pensive, as she sat dreading the reading of Henry's will.

His dry-as-dust solicitor would be calling on them the next day, to convey Henry's last wishes.

Gaston, having enjoyed a whole bottle of red wine to himself, was in ebullient form. 'Personally,' he mused, 'I usually have trouble staying awake when a solicitor is holding forth. However, the visit tomorrow is bound to prove entertaining.' The others choked on their wine. 'Furthermore,' he continued flippantly, unable to contain himself, 'I have various suggestions in mind for the inscription on Margot's headstone.'

Giselle frowned in his direction. 'Really, darling, one baby in the family is quite enough.' The level of hilarity went from bad to worse after that. 'So disrespectful after a funeral,' she said, and went to bed hiding her laughter.

They were woken next morning at 7am by the sound of tyres on gravel and other more indeterminate noises. Flora was in the garden gathering produce for the kitchen when she saw the lorry arrive with their delivery of heating oil.

She had primed the boiler and switched the heating to full on before the vehicle had even exited the gates at the end of the drive.

Henry's solicitor was expected late morning for the reading of the will. Inez had invited him to stay and join them for lunch, but he declined graciously as his diary was full that afternoon. Gaston thought that wise, as there was the likelihood of upsetting scenes when its contents were revealed. He couldn't wait to hear his late father-in-law's final wishes. *More dramas*, he thought, as he wandered off to find Flora.

She was leaving for Menton that afternoon to prepare for Gaston and Giselle's arrival at the weekend. He gave her flight tickets and enough money to see her through the week; her taxi to the airport was booked and instructions issued.

She was young and had not travelled widely. Gaston felt as protective of her as he would a daughter.

Speculation electrified the air, but Giselle's only concern was for her mother. If her father had bequeathed the estate elsewhere, it would represent a humiliating slap on the cheek for Inez.

'I will be so relieved when this is all over, then we can go home,' she remarked to Gaston as she was dressing. He took her in his arms and stroked her burgeoning tummy.

'Stretchy dresses soon, my darling,' he joked, his sultry eyes alight with love.

The weather was overcast and sullen, promising glimmers of dawn sunlight had receded into swirling sea fret. The raucous calls of the gulls overhead went unnoticed, as the occupants of the lodge were all seasoned coastal dwellers.

At the appointed hour, a black saloon car driven by Henry's solicitor glided up the drive. Gaston went out to welcome him, offering coffee or something stronger. Both were politely refused.

The man kept glancing back down the drive, as if he were expecting someone.

'Your gates are kept open, I trust, as I will need to leave immediately after the will has been read.' He muttered on about his full diary.

He's frightened of us, thought Gaston, amused at the prospect of scaring him further.

The solicitor was as described, dry as dust and seemingly twice as nervous. He was short, his bookish spectacles forming a canopy over his serious expression, and he walked with a shuffle and carried a large black leather briefcase.

Gaston led the way, thinking wryly that the man's last smile had probably been on his wedding night.

The solicitor bade them all good morning as he sat at the head of the table, furtively eyeing the remaining family members assembled around him.

They waited, wearing expectant expressions, whilst he carefully placed his paperwork in neat piles on the table before him. He had the air of a conductor facing an orchestra.

'Well' he said finally, giving each in turn a penetrating glance.

'Henry made his will shortly after his father died,' he announced. 'He added one bequest last year. Quite simply, he left his entire estate to Margot du Val. On her death, the estate would then pass to her daughter, Simone. In the untimely event of her death, the estate would be bequeathed to the local authority, to be used at their discretion for the good of the local community.' He paused. Everyone remained silent, Inez and Giselle were ashen-faced.

Simone's face glowed with triumph. If only Margot had been in the room to hear these validating words, the affirmation of his regard for them both. She had been right to insist on staying in England until her father's will had been read. Now her future had been decided for her.

Gaston shifted uncomfortably in his chair.

'The only exception, the solicitor continued, 'is a long case clock with a pearl face. I have a photograph of it here.'

Inez reeled with shock, unable to speak. Tears of latent anger and resentment welled inside her. After all these years, she had been disregarded and consigned to history. *He never loved me,* she thought.

The solicitor turned to Inez. 'Madame Roxberg,' he said, 'the accounts have revealed regular quarterly payments, since your marriage, from your father to your late husband, amounting in total to five million pounds.' He surveyed her with suspicion. 'Do you know why your father would pay such a large sum to your husband, rather than yourself?' He waited patiently for her reply.

Inez confirmed that she had no knowledge of the payments or their purpose. She further advised him that the clock had already been shipped to Menton for safe keeping, until after she had moved to Villefranche.

'Madame Roxberg, I can only offer you my sincere apologies, as those were your husband's last wishes.' He placed a copy of the will before her. 'This is your copy. If you have any further questions, please make an appointment with my assistant and we will do our utmost to help you.' A fleeting smile passed his lips. 'Now I must take my leave. Good day.' He stood up to leave.

Giselle, looking at Simone, asked the solicitor if Simone had had prior knowledge of her considerable inheritance.

'No, she had not. Your father's instructions were most emphatic. Neither she nor her mother knew of his intentions,' said the man.

They sat unsmiling, tense, and upset for Inez.

'Again, please accept my apologies. I have an appointment,' said the solicitor, impatient to leave.

Gaston showed him out, then locked the front door securely behind him.

Inez rose. 'Well, my darlings, Henry was determined that I have no part to play in the future prosperity of this house. Let's face it, he never loved me. He just wanted my father's money. I will cook supper,' she said with resignation.

Giselle let her go. In difficult times her mother usually headed for the kitchen to assuage her woes.

Iona had heard everything from the hall. When Inez entered the kitchen, she was at a loss as how to console her.

'Don't leave,' said Inez. 'Join me in a glass of wine and tell me everything. I need to know the truth.'

She gazed steadily into Iona's blushing face as the girl eagerly recounted the rumours regarding the monetary bribes paid to Henry for remaining distant from Inez.

Margot, from the outset, had learned of his dubious business dealings, and cleverly used subtle blackmail to trap and tether him. 'He knew there was no escape, not even when he married you,' Iona said.

'I should hate my father for this,' wailed Inez. 'His interference contributed to the ruin of my marriage. I am not a naïve child. Why didn't someone tell me? I could have curbed Margot, given the opportunity.'

Inez chopped and cooked, her mind clearing. She knew in her heart that time was running out. Never again would she repeat the mistakes that had shaped her life for so long and were still the emotional well of her unhappiness.

She was the stranger. Margot, even in death, had won.

Her unspeakable memories of Roxberg Gate would be sealed in the clock with a pearl face. Henry's parting gift; his only gift.

Gaston and Giselle were desperate to escape for a long beach walk, to feel the shingle beneath their boots, the salty air in their faces, in an attempt to evade the evil tentacles this house appeared to exude from every stone.

Suddenly regaining their sense of freedom from their own worries, however briefly, they behaved as newlyweds, seeking their pleasures at will.

They secreted themselves behind a cleft in the rock and kissed passionately. Leaving tantric practices aside, they freely indulged themselves in fingertip stimulation until their flames of pleasure were extinguished and their sensitive places cooled by the breeze.

Their intense, unconditional love for each other was an all-encompassing, infinite dream. Giselle vowed the child growing within her would never be allowed to diminish her marital bliss.

They were both conscious of a desire to leave this place of mischief and madness and return to the tranquil azure waters of their home town. Twilight was descending as they walked back along the beach.

Giselle's phone rang. She saw it was Simone calling, and blocked the call. Minutes later, she received a text from her, asking to meet urgently. Giselle, feeling guilty, invited her to dine with them that evening, then everyone would hear Simone's fascinating disclosures.

'In essence,' confided Simone, 'the lodge is practically worthless. The sea completely floods the cellars at high tide, and before long a storm will obliterate the whole building. We have lived trapped in terror for years, expecting the worst.

That is the reason Father didn't want you to inherit,' she said, looking at Inez. 'By preventing you from living here, he may have saved your life.'

They looked at each other in despair, not knowing what to make of Simone's revelations.

'My aim is to sell before oblivion descends,' she said.

Giselle still felt unable to tell Simone about her condition. Superstitiously, she felt it might contaminate the child by association.

Iona and her fiancé joined them that evening. Gaston was relieved to have found such entertaining, not to mention trustworthy, replacement members of staff so quickly, although he had forgotten to ask if they spoke French. When asked, they replied, 'Oui' in schoolchild French.

Two weeks had now passed since Gaston's arrival in Northumberland. He thought it felt like a year, and was longing to return home. Just two more days, then they would leave, never to return.

That night, Inez served her celebrated coq au vin with parmesan and basil potato wedges, seasonal greens, then lemon soufflé and red berries to follow. The feast was devoured at a leisurely pace over the remains of various vintages of French wine. Inez had set the scene. Great care was taken in laying the table with colour coordinated flowers, shells, and candles. Giselle lit a fire of logs and pine cones, their smoky scent drifted through the rooms.

She persisted in lamenting throughout dinner, 'Had Father advised Margot and Simone of their inheritance years ago, the need for deception, murder, and suicide would have been eradicated.'

She continued at length, 'How heartbreakingly pointless for everyone concerned. Their gratuitous greed has destroyed every shred of my family's honour.'

Gaston, turning to her, smiled ruefully. 'Darling, please, you are giving me indigestion.'

'Well, it's all fine and amusing for you,' she retorted, 'my family is in disgrace.'

They lingered at the table for two hours, talking and making plans for the future. Flora rang during the meal to say that she had arrived in Menton and was astonished to see sunshine and feel balmy breezes so late in the year.

This served to make Gaston more homesick, and he was almost exploding with impatience to leave by the morning.

Rising early, he embarked on his usual pre-breakfast run. The sharp air stung his cheeks, and plumes of warm breath escaped his lips as he effortlessly made his way along the shoreline. The sea, a glassy mirror, reflected a pinkish dawn.

He sat on a rock and mused for a while. He might have been the last human being alive on the planet that morning. No person, bird, or animal disturbed his equilibrium. He wondered if his unborn child would inherit the less palatable characteristics of Giselle's family. He would keep the child close and be an attentive father.

A frenzy of activity greeted him on his return. Iona was in the kitchen making pancakes and coffee. Giselle had meticulously packed most of her own belongings in a separate case, leaving Gaston to deal with his own garments, often referred to as a pile of jumble.

Inez had received an email from her builder, saying that her new home at Villefranche would be ready for occupation by the end of next week.

She clasped her hands together in relief. Her furniture and personal items from La Maison Bleu were scheduled for packing tomorrow and she would stay in a hotel until it arrived, so determined was she never to return to Honfleur.

She had asked her friend from Rouen to supervise the house clearance, rather than suffer the sorrow of looking at her own front doorstep and being forced to relive the memory of little Maude's sad demise.

By lunchtime, everyone was feeling quite exhausted. After taking an unaccustomed afternoon nap, they decided to explore the lodge en masse for the last time. Armed with torches and gloves, they began searching the towers for any unknown remnants of the past. Iona led the way, as she had over the years explored the many rooms and passages, some of which led to blank walls to confuse determined snoops.

Apart from their bedrooms and ground floor reception rooms, the lodge was virtually empty of furniture. The police had removed almost everything, and were now going through the lengthy process of returning the stolen items to their owners.

When they came upon the room which had previously held the German memorabilia, Giselle shuddered at the thought of her family being involved in such activities.

The wardrobe containing the uniforms had been removed, behind which a door had been revealed. They looked at each other.

'You first,' said Giselle, giving Gaston a playful push.

The studded oak door was unlocked, but the wood had swollen in the damp air and proved stubborn to open. With one immense push, and groaning on its hinges, the door swung open to reveal a large sitting room, with a bedroom and bathroom beyond.

The mullioned windows had vertical iron bars driven

into the latches to prevent them from being opened. The iron-framed bed had leather handcuffs on chains fixed to its frame. Inez ventured to open the cupboards and drawers and found diminutive, lace-trimmed, white cotton night and underwear. Red and blue velvet cloaks hung in the wardrobe with the name Adeline printed on labels inside their collars.

An inlaid walnut bureau stood under a window. It contained addressed writing paper and various coloured fountain pens, the ink having dried long ago. Personal letters to and from Henry were held fast in red and blue velvet ribbons with dried flowers underneath their bows. They were all neatly placed in the lower drawers under a red and blue silk scarf.

The family looked around askance at each other.

'Someone was imprisoned here,' said Inez.

Iona then remembered the rumours surrounding Henry's mother.

'Flora's grandmother told her of the strain of insanity which ran through the maternal side of the family,' she explained. 'Adeline was Henry's mother, and apparently there were occasions when she needed to be watched, due to her changeable nature.'

It was obvious that the woman had been confined here, as the rooms were so full of her personal items. Were it not for the cobwebs, one might imagine she had slept there recently.

'She took her own life when Henry was just six months old,' said Iona. 'His difficult birth sent her into a spiral of insanity, poor lady.'

Inez took the letters and photographs. 'I will keep them safe, as one day I may write the family's history,' she said.

Giselle was reluctant to leave the room. Her feeling of deep compassion for her long dead grandmother was intensified by her own pregnancy. Hearing more unsavoury details of Giselle's family history did nothing to calm Gaston's anxiety, as his wife was prone at times to volatility.

The following morning, they would all leave for France and the keys would be handed to Simone, leaving her alone in her inheritance.

Gaston decided that cooking was out of the question, as they had not restocked the kitchen, so promptly ordered a takeaway meal for everyone.

They communed in the kitchen to enjoy their meal, then retired early to prepare for the day they all been waiting for – their day of release into happiness.

Their goodbyes held no rancour or awkwardness, as Simone was also a victim of her late mother's pervasive greed. She was sorry to see them depart, leaving her alone and desolate. As she walked around the empty rooms, her footsteps echoed her loneliness.

'They have taken everything!' she screamed out loud.

As Gaston, Giselle, and Inez sped away down the drive to their new lives, no-one turned their head to look back.

Inez spent a pleasant but frenetic two weeks at the hotel closest to her new home, and watched as the final bespoke touches were completed to her satisfaction.

She familiarised herself with the delights of the town and services, and shopped in Nice for modernist items of furniture and any other frivolous items that caught her eye.

Her friend from Rouen was on hand to help and offer unwanted advice on the day she took possession of her, as yet, unnamed new residence.

After an exhausting week of arranging then rearranging furniture and ornaments, hanging drapery, and designing a mural scene for the staircase, she said goodbye to her friend.

Inez was relieved to be alone once more. She had projects in mind and needed to think. She looked thoughtfully at the packing case containing Henry's parting gift.

'When I release you, will you bring me joy or sadness?' she murmured to herself. Taking great care, she loosened the packing. The luminescence of the clock face shone out, falling on her like moonbeams, representing closure and a new beginning.

The intricate engraving of violets, their petals made from black pearls, glinted in the sunlight. 'Exquisite,' she said out loud. Taking the key from her handbag, she opened the body of the case.

Removing the debris, she began cleaning, not daring to touch the face.

She discovered a small silver plaque on the inside of the door, on which an inscription had been engraved with the words: *Adeline, my one true love, Henry.*

Inez was touched to tears; her father-in-law had finally shown himself to be a romantic at heart.

She cleaned purposefully, wiping away years of neglect, when suddenly the strong plinth around the base shot open. Inez was momentarily blinded by an aurora of sparkling prisms. A tray containing cut diamonds of all shapes and sizes lay before her, captured in a time capsule.

A small red envelope with her name written in her husband's hand lay waiting for her. Holding her breath, not daring to speculate as to its contents, she opened the envelope. Hidden inside was a card trimmed with red velvet. It read:

To Inez, my one true love, Henry.

To be continued........

Acknowledgments

My sincere thanks to Barbara Morris-Welsh, Barbara Matthews, Melissa Mailler-Yates, and Rosalie Williams, for their unwavering support.